Totally Bound Publishing

CW01086016

By T.A

The Four
Pesti
War
Famine
Death

The Beasor Chronicles
Gypsies
Tramps

Home
No Going Home
Home of His Own
Wishing for a Home
Leaving Home
Home Sweet Home

Rags to Riches
Remove the Empty Spaces
Close the Distance
Following His Footsteps
Anywhere Tequila Flows

Every Shattered Dream
Part One
Part Two
Part Three
Part Four

Out of Light into Darkness
From Slavery to Freedom
The Vanguard
Two for One
Stealing Life

Anthologies
Unconventional At Best: Ninja Cupcakes
Unconventional in Atlanta: His Last Client

What's his Passion?
Mountains to Climb

By Jambrea Jo Jones

Stand to Attention: On the Home Front
Lasso Lovin': Forever Changed

By Stephani Hecht

Dragon's Soul
Dragon's Eye

In the Crease
Redemption or Burn

Anthologies
Unconventional at Best: Fan-Tastic
Unconventional in Atlanta: Slippery When Wet

Collections
Heart Attack: Going With My Heart

By Amber Kell

Supernatural Mates
From Pack to Pride
A Prideful Mate
A Prideless Man
Nothing To Do With Pride
Talan's Treasure
More Than Pride
Protecting His Pride
Overcoming His Pride

Cowboy Lovin'
Tyler's Cowboy
Robert's Rancher

Yearning Love
Taking Care of Charlie
Protecting Francis
In Broussard's Care

Matchmaker, Matchmaker
Switching Payne

Anthologies
Unconventional at Best: Convention Confusion
Unconventional in Atlanta: Blown Away

Collections
Heart Attack: My Subby Valentine
Scared Stiff: Protecting His Soul

By Devon Rhodes

Vampires & Mages & Werewolves Oh My!
A Pint Light
Through the Red Door
Locke, Stock and Barrel

Wet Your Whistle
Christmas of White

Anthologies
Gaymes: Rough Riders
His Hero: A Ring and A Promise
Unconventional at Best: Rough Awakening
Unconventional in Atalanta: Out of Service

Collections
Homecoming: A Detour Home
Feral: Pride and Joey

AN UNCONVENTIONAL CHICAGO ANTHOLOGY

NO BRAVERY
T.A. CHASE

LOVE DON'T DIE
JAMBREA JO JONES

PASSION UNDER FIRE
STEPHANI HECHT

GANGING UP ON LOVE
AMBER KELL

BONFIRE HEART
DEVON RHODES

An Unconventional Chicago Anthology
ISBN # 978-1-78430-158-3
No Bravery ©Copyright T.A. Chase 2014
Love Don't Die ©Copyright Jambrea Jo Jones 2014
Passion Under Fire ©Copyright Stephani Hecht 2014
Ganging Up on Love ©Copyright Amber Kell 2014
Bonfire Heart ©Copyright Devon Rhodes 2014
Cover Art by Posh Gosh ©Copyright July 2014
Interior text design by Claire Siemaszkiewicz
Totally Bound Publishing

Published in 2014 by Totally Bound Publishing, Newland House, The Point, Weaver Road, Lincoln, LN6 3QN, United Kingdom.

Totally Bound Publishing is an imprint of Total-E-Ntwined Limited.

NO BRAVERY

T.A. Chase

Dedication

To all the ladies who have joined me on this journey through a different Chicago, I'm glad you were with me. And to all those who fight to make the world a better place.

Chapter One

"I wasn't fucking crazy when you threw my naïve ass into the mental asylum, brother dearest," Farris muttered as he walked out of City Hall. He had finally been released from meetings with his brother, the head of the O'Laughlin gang. His family was one of the forces behind the people who ran the city. "But having to go to these meetings might just push me over the edge."

Since Farris was wrapped up in his one-sided conversation and wasn't watching where he was going, he bumped into someone. He glanced up to growl then realized he'd run into the Deputy Mayor.

"My apologies, Mr O'Laughlin. I wasn't paying attention to where I was going," Thierry Alexander said, even though they both knew it was Farris' fault.

He dredged up some courtesy and said, "We both need to watch where we're going, Deputy Mayor."

Alexander studied him for a moment. *Probably waiting to see if I'll go mental on him*, Farris snarled in his head. Outwardly, he kept his usual complacent expression.

"Ah, Thierry, there you are. The meeting's about to start." The Mayor took Alexander by the arm then started to drag him into the building.

"Have a good day, Mr O'Laughlin," Alexander said before disappearing with the Mayor.

Farris snorted as he continued on his way to where his car was parked at the curb. His driver held open the back door and Farris climbed in. He had no respect for the politicians who suckled at the teat of the gangs who really ran the city. Every gang gave the sycophants in City Hall a lot of money to pass laws that enriched them while bankrupting the others who called Chicago home.

Chicago had been sectioned into wards and the citizens were forced stay within their own among those of their own economic and ethnic backgrounds. The gangs ruled from City Hall and took advantage of everyone's fear.

But for a minute there, Farris had thought Alexander seemed different from the others. Maybe it was as simple as the fact that Alexander had acknowledged Farris when most went out of their way to ignore him.

"Spending thirteen years in a mental hospital does tend to make one invisible to others," Farris muttered.

"What was that, sir?" his driver asked as he climbed into the front seat.

It wasn't the question that caught Farris' fractured attention, but the fact the man asked it at all. Glancing up, he met a pair of dark green eyes reflected in the rear view mirror. They didn't look familiar and neither did the face they were a part of. Farris couldn't remember what his driver actually looked like.

He'd be the first to admit that he was rather uninterested in the world he lived in. The people who inhabited it were even less interesting. Only one person existed for him and that was his brother, Ralph — the man he planned on destroying.

"The bastard has to pay for what he's done," Farris spoke aloud while still staring at his driver.

"I'm sure he'll get what's coming to him, sir." The guy flashed a bright white smile at him, yet Farris noticed a crooked incisor and a chipped front tooth.

"You're not my driver." He reached to grab the handgun he wore in a holster under his jacket.

"I'm your new driver, Mr O'Laughlin. Darien Shaunessy. The King hired me." Darien tipped his head.

"The King." Farris grunted. "Utterly ridiculous title. The bloody bastard got quite pretentious while I was gone. Thinks he's fucking royalty now."

Darien didn't react to Farris' outburst. He just kept watching him.

"What happened to my other driver?" He frowned as he tried to remember the man's name. "Where is he?"

"*She* was transferred to a different position, sir." Darien's lips quirked up at the corners like he was fighting not to smile.

"My last driver was a woman?" Farris couldn't believe he hadn't noticed that.

Admittedly, women weren't even blips on his radar. He didn't sleep with them, so most got regulated into background scenery. Also, he couldn't remember her ever saying anything to him. Darien was the first driver he'd had who'd talked to him since he'd come back five years ago.

There wasn't anything Farris could do about the new driver. Once his brother had spoken, the order was sacrosanct and only death could change it.

"I suppose my dear brother's secretary already gave you my itinerary for the day."

"Yes, Mr O'Laughlin." Darien turned the car on.

"Then let's go, man. The sooner we get the money collected, the sooner I can go home and stop pretending like I enjoy my life."

Taking a deep breath, Farris got control of his anger and his tongue. No one cared what he thought or felt. They were paid to ignore him, and in the five years since he'd been allowed to return to the fold, he hadn't made any friends. Not that he wanted any. Last time he'd cared about someone, his brother had killed him and destroyed any proof he'd existed.

It had been well thought out and executed. Farris had to give his brother props for that. Ralph had wanted the 'throne' and had figured out the best way to take it. Just as Farris had been set to take over control of the O'Laughlin family's enterprises, his younger brother had taken him out in a brilliant coup, and he'd spent thirteen years in a mental hospital.

"I wasn't crazy then," he repeated.

Darien shot a quick glance into the mirror, probably to check if Farris was talking to him. Farris shook his head as he stared out of the window. He'd been trusting when he was younger, but one thing those thirteen years had taught him was not to trust anyone. Everyone was out to get him, and he was doing his best to keep from getting stabbed in the back again.

They pulled up in front of the first store, causing Farris to draw in a deep breath. He hated going to the businesses and collecting the protection money. He understood why his brother had given him this job. It was the lowest position that Farris could take, but also because of his scary past, it made the storeowners more likely to make the payments without arguing.

If they did argue, Farris had Darien to convince them following the laws was the most prudent thing. He frowned as he stepped from the car.

"How did my former driver convince people to pay me?" While he couldn't bring her face up in his memory, he was pretty sure she hadn't been that big of a woman. "She wasn't that big. Unless I'm thinking of someone else," he qualified.

"She was trained in some kind of martial arts, I believe," Darien said as they approached the entrance to the store. He pulled the door open so Farris could walk through. "Don't worry. I'm just as skilled as she was."

Stopping, Farris trailed his gaze from the top of Darien's dark brown curls to the toes of his shiny black boots. Along the way he cataloged the man's broad shoulders and wide chest. Something told Farris the suit Darien wore had to be tailored to fit the man's large, muscular body. There was a discreet bump at Darien's side that informed Farris that his driver was armed as well.

Letting his gaze drop below Darien's waist, Farris eyed the rather impressive bulge behind the man's zipper. Looked like a gun wasn't the only thing his new driver was packing.

A clearing throat brought Farris' gaze back up to Darien's face. The driver winked at him and Farris blinked, shocked at the familiarity of it. *Who does he think he is? He's not my friend who gets to wink at me like he knows what I'm thinking.*

He scowled at Darien before turning back to look at the storeowner. Not speaking, he just stared at the man. It wasn't like the guy didn't know what Farris was doing there. He raised an eyebrow when the other man started to open his mouth.

"I know you're not planning to tell Mr O'Laughlin you don't have the money for the payment," Darien spoke up from where he stood behind Farris.

Farris fought off the need to move so Darien wasn't breathing on the back of his neck. He hated having anyone where he couldn't see them. Too many times bad things had happened when someone snuck up behind him at the hospital. Yet he couldn't step to either side because that would be showing weakness and he couldn't let Darien see him as fragile.

Fragile would get him killed and he couldn't allow that to happen. Crazy and anti-social got him left mostly to himself, which suited his purpose perfectly.

"No. Of course not. I have it right here." The owner held out a white envelope.

Darien reached around Farris to take it, and Farris shrank from the brush of Darien's sleeve against his shoulder. He gritted his teeth. *One more mark against my brother. Making me come to these places when he could just send a man like Darien.*

He didn't take the payment from Darien to check it, knowing his hands were shaking too much, and besides, no one was stupid enough to cheat the O'Laughlins. People had a habit of dying when that happened. He listened as Darien opened the package then shuffled through the bills.

"It's all there."

"Of course it is. We'll be stopping by next month." Farris slid to the side to avoid running into Darien before walking out of the store. The footsteps following him unnerved him even more, but he refused to look back.

Stopping at the car, he waited until Darien joined him to open the door. Yet he stayed where he was without looking at the man.

"Sir?"

"I'm done for the day, Shaunessy. Take me back to my apartment," he ordered, having decided he didn't want to do what his brother planned for him at the moment.

"We still have eight places to go before we can stop," Darien reminded him.

Farris shook his head. "You have eight more places to go. I'm not important in this little racket my brother has going. They'll give you the money just as easily as they hand it to me."

Darien grunted, but didn't say anything else. He simply kept the door open, waiting for Farris to move. Finally Farris climbed into the car then settled back against the leather. He knew what Darien's orders were—taking Farris with him as he continued to collect the rest of the payments before returning Farris to his apartment, all while making sure Farris hadn't gone off the deep end again.

Ralph didn't want Farris left alone, not even for a single moment, so Farris' driver lived with him. Having lived for all those years with someone always watching him, Farris never paid any attention to the person who shared his space. Which was obvious, since he hadn't figured out that his former driver was a woman.

Darien slid behind the wheel, but before he started the car, he turned to look at Farris. "You know what my orders are."

"Yes. I'm well aware what your orders are, but I don't give a flying fuck what my brother wants." Farris shrugged, not taking his gaze from the people passing by on the street. "It's not my concern. It's cold out, and I want to go home."

"Cold? It'll be around seventy degrees by this afternoon." Darien sounded confused.

Farris didn't want to talk about why seventy was cold to him. "Yes. Take me home, Darien, and I will go with you later to drop the money off to my brother."

Darien faced forward before starting the car. He pulled out into traffic and Farris relaxed slightly, though he tugged his coat tighter around his body. After five years, one would think he was used to the weather, but he'd never adjusted and during the winter, he rarely left his apartment.

"I'll drop you off at the apartment, though I have to walk you to your door," Darien informed him.

Farris scowled. "I'm not a child. I can make my way from the street into my place without a chaperone. I'm not going to have a fit or a mental lapse and kill people."

Snorting, Darien said, "I don't really care if you do or not, sir. I'm going to do at least a little bit of what my orders are."

"Whatever."

"I'm glad to hear you're concerned about my job."

Shooting a look at the mirror, Farris jolted when he met Darien's green eyes for a second before his driver went back to watching the road. "Why should I be concerned about your job?"

"Because I could lose it if the King finds out I'm not doing what he wants me to do."

Farris shrugged. "And why would that be my problem?"

"You really are a bastard, aren't you?" Darien didn't sound all that shocked, actually.

"My father was married to my mother when they had me, so no, I'm not a bastard. I'm sure everyone warned you about me before you took this job." Farris studied his hands where they lay in his lap. They weren't shaking anymore, but he clenched them tight enough to make the knuckles go white. "Just do your job, Shaunessy. The worse that will happen is you'll be reassigned somewhere else. I do think you're my third driver since I was released."

From the corner of his eyes, Farris saw Darien shake his head. "I'm actually your sixth driver since you returned to Chicago."

"Huh? Well, as I assume all of them are doing some other job, then you can see that I won't murder you in your sleep at least." Farris ran through the years he'd been back and couldn't bring up images of any of his drivers' faces except for Darien's. Maybe it was because none of them had talked to him or that he'd never really acknowledged them one way or another. They were simply there, like the nurses and orderlies who had worked at the asylum he'd been incarcerated in.

Darien sighed and Farris wasn't sure if it sounded like he was exasperated or disbelieving. "Yes, they all have different jobs. Did you know they requested other placements?"

Farris laughed even as he shivered. "Am I supposed to be upset or hurt by that?"

"I guess not." Darien must have turned the heat up because a burst of warmth washed over Farris.

Silence fell over them, and Farris slipped his thumb under his shirtsleeve to start rubbing it over the rough scar bisecting his left forearm. He needed to get home, surround himself with things that were his while locking the door to keep others out. Farris hated being out in the city. Hated everything that reminded him of someone he wanted to forget but had never been able to get out of his head.

When the door next to him opened and cooler air rushed into the car, Farris jerked. He'd zoned out for the rest of the trip. He climbed out then headed into the building. The doorman didn't greet him, just stood out of the way. Farris walked onto the elevator before turning to face the doors. He wanted to ignore Darien's presence beside him, but he couldn't.

Darien stood so close to him that Farris could feel the heat rolling from the man's body. He wanted to move until he was pressed into Darien's side, if only for the chance to absorb some of Darien's heat. *You need to get this obsession with heat under control. It can be used as a weakness against you and you can't be weak. Not now when you're so close to achieving your goal.*

He tried to inhale quietly, not wishing for Darien to hear and think he was upsetting Farris. No one could know or guess anything that might bother him. He needed to appear unflappable and unemotional. His brother had wanted him broken before he came back and that was how Farris was going to present himself.

When the elevator stopped at his floor, Farris strolled from it like he hadn't a care in the world. He allowed Darien to unlock the door before he stepped in. He turned to look at his driver.

"You can go and collect the money from the other businesses. I don't plan on leaving here for the rest of the day." He started to shut the door in Darien's face.

Darien pressed his hand against the wood to stop its forward progress. "I do expect you to be here, sir. If I'm going to fudge the rules for you, then you better do me a solid and keep your ass in this apartment."

Farris reared his head back. "Do you a solid? I'm not one of your buddies, Shaunessy. You work for me. Please try to remember that."

After whirling around, he walked away, biting his lip to keep from saying anything more. He wouldn't get in an argument with Darien. Arguing led to punishments and he'd had more than enough of those in his past. He stripped off his overcoat before hanging it up in the closet. The soft click of the latch informed him that Darien had shut the door. Taking a chance, he glanced over to the foyer, but Darien wasn't there and Farris hoped that meant the man had gone to take care of the collections for the day.

He checked the thermostat and nudged the temp up another degree. Rubbing his arms, he shuffled to his bedroom where he undressed then put his dirty clothes in their designated baskets. His suits and dress shirts went to the dry cleaners while his weekly maid service did the rest of his clothes.

After digging through his dresser, he grabbed some clothes to change into after his shower. He'd clean up then do some research. He was getting close to getting the last bit of information he needed to knock his brother from his throne.

* * * *

Four hours later, Darien walked into the apartment he'd just moved into earlier that day. He hadn't been sure about the arrangement when he'd first been given the assignment. His fellow enforcers had been quick to share all the gossip they knew about Farris O'Laughlin, the King's older brother.

When the O'Laughlin family had first hired Darien, he'd done some digging. It wasn't often that a younger brother took over as head of the family, but it seemed like Farris had suffered some kind of breakdown days before he was supposed to take over for his old man.

Now, Darien wasn't a betting man, but if he was, he'd lay odds that Ralph had done something to help his brother over the edge. The bitterness and anger he'd heard in Farris' voice early that day told him there was a history between the brothers that hid in the shadows.

Stepping into the penthouse was like getting hit by a wall of heat. Sweat beaded his forehead as he removed his coat to hang it in the closet next to Farris'. He unbuttoned his cuffs before rolling up his sleeves.

"Fuck. It's like a sauna in here," he muttered, making a beeline for the thermostat. He swore when he saw the temp. "Mr O'Laughlin, why is the heat on and why the fuck is it set at seventy-eight degrees?"

The city was mid-way through spring and the temperatures had been steadily rising over the last couple of weeks. Darien had never had the heat that high in his dingy loft, not even during the coldest days of winter. He reached out to turn it down.

"Don't touch it."

His mouth dropped open when he turned to find Farris standing in the middle of the living room wearing sweatpants, socks and a heavy sweatshirt. Darien could see sweat on the man's skin, yet he seemed to be shivering as well. He remembered seeing Farris shiver in the car.

"Are you sick, sir? I'll call a doctor, or maybe I should take you to the hospital." Darien reached for his phone.

"*No!*" Farris shouted and Darien froze, phone halfway to his mouth. "I will never go to another hospital, even if I'm dying of the plague."

"Okay, but you don't look so good." Darien returned his phone to his pocket. "Maybe if you change into some shorts and a T-shirt and I'll turn the heat down a little, you'll feel better."

Hell, he could turn it off and it would be more than warm enough for them. He reached for the thermostat again.

"I told you no. The temperature stays where it is. There is nothing that will ever make me feel better." Farris folded his arms over his chest and glared at Darien.

While Farris wore his usual blank expression, Darien looked closer to see a hint of panic in the eyes that one of his former drivers had described as chips of ice blue diamonds. Darien had seen that coldness earlier that day when Farris had come out of City Hall after a round of meetings with his brother. There'd been not a shred of kindness or friendliness on his face the entire time they'd been together before Darien had dropped the man off. Yet there seemed to be a crack in Farris' façade and somehow it had to do with being warm.

"All right. I'll leave it there, but you're going to have to deal with me walking around in a lot less clothing than I'm wearing now." Darien wasn't sure if he meant that as a threat or a promise.

If he hadn't been watching so closely, he would've never seen Farris relax just a little. His new job was going to be harder than he'd ever imagined. Whatever connection Farris had once had to his family and the world seemed to have broken during his time away and his breakdown. Maybe Farris hadn't been the best choice when he'd picked whom to use as his entrance into the O'Laughlin family.

He'd promised Cesar, his oldest friend, to find out all he could about who Tomas' mystery lover had been and why that man had turned on him so terribly all those years ago. Cesar was Tomas' cousin and had never given up on trying to figure out where he'd gone. He figured being the driver/bodyguard for the oldest O'Laughlin brother would get him into the inner sanctum. Too bad Ralph wanted nothing to do with him even though he kept Farris under twenty-four-hour surveillance.

Farris waved his hand in a vague *whatever* gesture. "I couldn't care less what you wear, Shaunessy. Walk around fucking naked. I won't even notice."

Darien wanted to laugh because he'd seen the way Farris had eyed his crotch and there had been a little flare of interest in the man's gaze before he'd closed down. Walking around bare-assed might be a way to get Farris to pay more attention to him, but Darien had a feeling it wouldn't get Farris to trust him anytime soon.

"Have you eaten yet?" He strolled over to the kitchen as he asked.

"What time is it?" Farris sounded distracted and Darien glanced over his shoulder to see Farris staring out of the large window taking up one whole wall of the living room. He no longer had his arms crossed, but he was rubbing his thumb over the sleeve of his left wrist.

"Around six. I thought I'd make us some dinner." He opened up the fridge and gaped at the empty shelves. After shutting the door, he went around to check all the cupboards. They were all empty. "Why don't you have any food in here?"

There had only been two plates, a set of silverware for two people and two glasses. Darien went out into the living room before doing a slow three-sixty, studying the entire open floor plan. Aside from the furniture, there was nothing on the walls or shelves. The place was barren, like no one lived there.

"There isn't food?" Farris frowned. "I remember eating something last night. At least I think it was last night."

"Do you cook?" Darien figured he already knew the answer to his question, but felt like he had to ask.

Farris shook his head. "No. I just eat what they give me."

'What they give me' was an interesting statement and Darien would've liked to explore that further, but Farris shot him a glance.

"Are you a good cook?"

Shocked that Farris had asked any kind of question, Darien nodded. "I had to be. My mom was a single mother, and when she was working, I had to feed my siblings."

Farris turned away and Darien knew he'd lost him somewhere during the explanation. The man wasn't interested in anything that didn't directly concern him. Why Darien had had to learn to cook had nothing to do with him.

"They aren't good cooks. Everything is so bland and white. Why is it always white?" Farris shook his head as if the question had been burning in his head for some time.

Darien truly didn't know what Farris was talking about. It was time to make a decision and he had a feeling Farris wasn't going to do that for him.

"How about I order some food and have it delivered?" Darien tugged his phone out of his pocket. "Do you have a favorite takeout place around here?"

The look he got from Farris was filled with sardonic disbelief. "Shaunessy, if I don't remember what time it is or when I've eaten last, what makes you think I'd have a favorite restaurant?"

Darien deserved that. "Is there anything you don't want to eat?"

"As long as it isn't white, I couldn't really care less what you order." Farris appeared to be done with the conversation as he wandered toward the back of the penthouse. "I probably won't eat it anyway."

Why had he bothered to ask Farris anything? It was obvious the man lived in a world all on his own and he only occasionally stopped by to visit with the rest of them. It was going to be quite an interesting time, but Darien wasn't ready to call it quits yet.

Chapter Two

Darien opened the back door of the car to let Farris out, watching as Farris stood then tugged at his cuffs. Well, it wasn't really a tug. More like Farris rubbing his thumb over his left wrist again. It was a habit of Farris' Darien had noticed the night before. He didn't know whether Farris realized he even did it.

They headed toward City Hall, and Farris shivered, wrapping his coat tighter around him. Darien didn't understand how the man could be cold when it was around seventy and promised to get warmer before the day was over. Last night, he'd slept naked and without any covers because he couldn't take the heat. He had turned the heat down after Farris had gone to his room, but since he hadn't wanted to upset Farris again, he'd still kept it rather high. So in the end, it hadn't helped Darien get a good night's sleep.

Then there was the whole food issue. He wasn't sure how it was possible for Farris not to have any food in his place. Darien had been surprised at how upset he'd become at that fact. Also, the idea that Farris didn't remember when he'd eaten last angered Darien.

He wasn't angry at Farris, but at the people who were supposed to be watching the man. It didn't matter that Farris was cold and sometimes cruel. It was obvious he couldn't take care of himself and his helplessness touched Darien.

It was a feeling he'd never thought he'd have for a member of one of the families, especially the O'Laughlins, who had caused Tomas' disappearance. He shouldn't have sympathy for any of them, yet he couldn't help thinking that whatever had happened to Farris before he came back to Chicago five years ago had damaged something deep inside the man. Darien couldn't help wanting to help Farris learn how to survive in this world that Farris seemed out of touch with.

Farris' not eating would explain why he was so slender, almost to the point of being too skinny. The long-sleeved shirts and suits did a lot to hide the physical signs, but Darien was trained to observe. He noticed Farris' high cheekbones seemed razor sharp in his gaunt face, which helped with the whole 'emotionally dead and unstable' look Farris wore constantly.

"Farris, come on. We can't start these meetings without you," Ralph O'Laughlin—'King' as he commanded everyone to call him—shouted down the corridor as they approached the building.

"There are times when I wonder which would be better—trying to kill myself again or killing him," Farris muttered.

Darien didn't react, unsure if he was supposed to have heard that or not. He escorted Farris to the room where the King stood.

"I'll be here to drive you home when you're done," Darien informed Farris.

"I hope you have more fun than I'll be having the next couple of hours." Farris did his thumb thing again while his gaze went colder than usual and his face went blank.

Once the door closed behind them, Darien headed to the coffee shop a block from City Hall where all the O'Laughlin enforcers gathered. All the families had their own turf around the Hall. They all needed a place where their employees could hang out while they robbed Chicago blind behind laws passed by politicians who were for sale.

There was a rumor going around the populace that a new immigration bill that was being passed wasn't the sweeping reform the lawmakers were spinning it to be. In fact, some were saying that it was a way for the families to clean Chicago of the riff-raff and the poor. It was rumored that certain ethnic groups could find themselves deported to camps or different states.

While Darien was worried about the bigger picture the bill represented, he was also interested in finding out the truth about Tomas' disappearance, and to do that, he had to get close to the O'Laughlin leaders. Cesar, Darien's best friend and former lover, had told him that Tomas had been involved with a top level O'Laughlin member before every record of his existence was erased. Then Tomas had appeared in the company of sex slavers three years ago, and when he truly disappeared after that time, Cesar needed to know if he was dead or not. He wanted to know if the O'Laughlins were responsible for Tomas' slavery.

After picking up his order, he glanced around the crowded shop and spotted Alyssa, Farris' former driver. As he sat at her table, he grinned at her scowl.

"How's the new assignment?" He sipped his coffee.

Alyssa shrugged. "Better than dealing with crazy O'Laughlin. You started driving him yesterday. Haven't had enough of the silent treatment yet?"

"What's up with that? It's like I don't even exist." He could lie with the best of them, though he was pretty sure that the way Farris was reacting to him wasn't his normal reaction.

She leaned over to pat his arm. "Don't worry. It's his usual MO. None of us exist to him. You know, I talked to some of the guys who were here back before he left, and they said he wasn't nearly this bad."

"What happened? Where did he go?" Darien hadn't really been able to find out much information about that.

"Not sure, except the gossip is that he went crazy. Started accusing King of killing some guy, but when people went to investigate, the guy didn't exist. How can his brother kill a person who wasn't real? It's like murdering your invisible friend." Alyssa snorted. "They say he freaked out and King had no recourse except getting him admitted to a mental hospital somewhere up in Wisconsin. King was devastated because he had to do that. He'd always looked up to Farris."

Darien managed to stop the instinctive roll of his eyes. Like anyone believed King was torn up because of having to commit his brother and take over the family. "You drink the Kool-Aid when you signed on to drive for them?"

She looked affronted by his calling her bullshit, but Darien didn't care. Farris might not have been the nicest person before he went away, and God knew he was an absolute bastard now that he was back, but he hadn't deserved to lose his freedom and his mind because of his brother's play for power.

"If you think King cared anything about his brother, then you've let them brainwash you. King made his play for the throne and did what he had to do to get his older brother out of the way." Darien shrugged at her horrified stare. "I'm calling it like it is and they can't arrest me for speaking my mind. At least not yet, anyway."

"You're fucking crazy yourself, Shaunessy. Maybe you'll last longer with Farris than the rest of us did. That man is scary crazy."

A thought hit him, and he looked at Alyssa. "Did he ever get angry when you worked with him?"

"He doesn't get angry. I've never seen him yell or scream. He goes still and stares at you, but it's not for intimidation or anything like that. I truly believe he's running through all the ways he'd kill you."

Darien grunted, but said nothing. He didn't want to interrupt her.

"Then once he's killed you a hundred different ways in his mind, he'll smile before walking away. And you're so unnerved by the whole thing, you don't remember what you'd been talking about that put the whole process in motion." Alyssa shuddered.

"Does he do that with King?"

"It's worse. He looks at Mr O'Laughlin like that when King doesn't realize Farris is looking at him. When King looks over, Farris wears a smile that's as cold as the wind off the lake during winter. You just know that given a chance, Farris would cut his brother's heart out while it was still beating and offer it up to whatever demon Farris worships. Mr O'Laughlin thinks those years in the hospital broke Farris, but I think they created a monster far worse than he's ever imagined."

And Darien thought the enforcer had read too many serial killer books. Then he remembered Farris' comment before going into the meetings about killing himself or King. The hatred in Farris' voice told him that given half a chance of success, Farris would take a knife to his brother and possibly would cut out his heart, assuming King had one.

He decided to turn the topic to something else, no longer interested in gossiping about Farris. Darien should've known gossip and rumors were never entirely true. Oh there was some hidden grain of truth in almost every rumor, but it took so long to dig it out that it was never worth the time.

But something nudged his brain and he asked, "Do you remember if this invisible friend had a name?"

A wrinkle appeared in the middle of Alyssa's forehead as she seemed to be thinking. "I want to say it was some Hispanic name. Pablo, Miguel." She shook her head. "Actually, neither of those sounds right."

"Could it have been Tomas?" He didn't want to get his hopes up.

She pursed her lips then exhaled loudly. "It could've been. To be honest, I wasn't paying all that much attention when they were talking about him because he didn't exist. Farris made him up."

"Hmm..." Darien wasn't so sure Farris had made anything up, except for saying Ralph had killed Tomas because Darien knew the truth about that. He had to think of a way to bring up the events leading up to Farris' stay in the asylum, and wouldn't that be a pleasant conversation?

Another driver came to sit with them, and Darien settled back in his chair, letting the conversation drift around him as he worked to organize his thoughts. If

Farris had been Tomas' lover, Darien doubted he was in on the whole being sold to slavers thing. Not if he'd freaked out enough for Ralph to feel justified in calling him crazy. A man cold enough to treat his lover like an object wouldn't throw a fit about it. He'd continue on like nothing had happened.

Just taking one look at Farris told Darien the man had suffered and was still suffering from whatever had gone down all those years ago. *Could all of the issues Farris seems to have stem from that one moment in his life?* Darien wasn't a psychologist, so coming up with a diagnosis was beyond him.

His phone buzzed, and he glanced at the screen as he stood. It was Farris. Something must have gone wrong because the meetings had several more hours to go. After finishing his drink, he tossed the cup in the trash on the way out of the door. Darien strolled as quickly as possible to where he saw Farris standing next to the curb.

Farris had his arms wrapped around his waist and he shivered almost violently while sweat gleamed on his forehead. Darien thought about touching him then changed his mind when he concluded that Farris was dancing on the edge of a breakdown. *Emotional or mental?* Darien decided it didn't matter.

"Are you ready to go home, sir?" He opened the car door before meeting Farris' gaze.

His eyes were blank and his face pale. His jaw was taut like he was gritting his teeth to keep from screaming. Darien laid his hand on Farris' shoulder for just a second, hoping to encourage the man to move forward.

Farris dove into the backseat then curled up by the other door. Darien shot a look over his shoulder and saw King standing at the top of the steps. King smirked at him then turned back to walk inside.

Anger welled in Darien. What had O'Laughlin done to Farris to get the man to react that way? Why did he continue to torment his brother? It wasn't like Farris had the resources to do anything to harm him, no matter how much Farris wanted to.

He slammed the door shut then climbed in behind the wheel. "Don't worry, sir. I'll get you back to your place. You can get warm there."

"I want to rip his heart out," Farris said from the back.

Darien glanced behind him to see Farris staring straight ahead and while he still shivered, he seemed more under control. "I understand that, sir, but you can't do anything here."

"Take me home, so I can work on knocking him off the throne he stole from me."

"All right."

Had Farris got control of himself that quickly? Or had it all been an act for Ralph? He took another quick look in the backseat to see Farris rubbing his left wrist again. Only this time the sleeve was rolled up and Darien could see the ragged scar running from where his hand met his wrist almost all the way up to his elbow.

'Trying to kill myself again' rolled through Darien's mind and a light bulb went off. At some point in the thirteen years he'd been gone, Farris had reached the point where living hadn't been worth the pain anymore. He obviously hadn't had anyone to help him through the darkness, but at least they'd managed to save him from actually ending his life.

Without saying anything, he faced forward to start the car. Darien pulled into traffic, wanting to get back to Farris' place before Farris rubbed his skin raw. He might not act as upset as he had seemed, but Darien had a feeling Farris was struggling to hold on to whatever kept him from shattering.

Nothing was said until they were inside the apartment. Darien took Farris' coat as the man stripped out of it. Farris headed straight toward his room.

"I'm going to go get some groceries so I can make us something for dinner. Plus I want some coffee."

Farris flapped his hand at him, and for some reason, Darien felt proud that he'd acknowledged him even while focusing on something in his own mind. After stepping outside into the hallway, he took a deep breath. It was only his second day driving Farris O'Laughlin around Chicago and already he was exhausted. Maybe that was part of the reason why his other drivers asked to be reassigned.

Darien wasn't about to give up yet. He had a job to do and he'd put up with whatever he had to in order to get it done.

* * * *

When Darien went to bed later that night, he left the door open, not wanting to give Farris a chance to sneak out during the night. He confessed it was useless paranoia because Farris wasn't about to leave his apartment. Not when he considered it his safe place.

At some point, a noise brought Darien out of his dream and he stared up at the ceiling, trying to place it in his mind. There it was again, and this time it sounded like a whimper. Swiping his hand across his face to remove some of the sweat, Darien argued with himself on whether he should go check on Farris or not.

If he did, more than likely Farris would tell him to go to hell. When yet another whimper—louder this time—broke through the darkness, Darien couldn't stay in his bed.

After leaving his room, he stalked down the hallway toward Farris'. He'd been in there earlier in the evening, working to convince Farris to eat something. It hadn't gone well. Farris had been focused on something else and Darien had been distracted by how empty the room was. Just like the rest of the apartment, the walls and shelves were bare. The only thing on Farris' dresser was a watch.

All his clothes must have been neatly tucked away because there wasn't even a stray sock on the floor. His bed was piled high with blankets. Darien had counted at least six, with several more folded up in the corner of the room.

Now as he entered, all he could see of the man was the very top of Farris' head, his ginger curls damp from sweat. Darien tried to work out how to approach Farris without surprising him. Farris struck Darien as being the kind of man who would have a shank under his pillow and wouldn't hesitate to use it against someone.

Standing at the foot of the bed, Darien called out quietly, "Farris. Hey, man, wake up."

Farris rolled under the covers, but didn't come out. Darien held his breath as he reached out to shake Farris' foot.

"Farris. It's just a dream." He shook it harder.

"Don't fucking touch me!" Farris shouted as he shot up, holding a knife pointed straight at Darien.

Darien raised his hands shoulder high, showing that he was unarmed. Thank God Farris had left a light on. "Farris, it's me. Darien. I'm not here to hurt you."

"Darien," Farris murmured, letting the knife drop onto the blankets. "Why are you here?"

Farris shivered while sweat dripped from his chin. Before Darien could say anything, Farris yanked the blankets up to cover his body as much as possible.

"I can't get warm. Why is it so cold in here? You didn't touch the thermostat, did you?" he accused Darien.

"No, sir. I haven't touched it all day. You do know it's not cold in here at all. In fact, you're sweating." Darien felt compelled to point that out.

Farris exhaled as he reached up to touch his forehead then brought his fingers down to where he could look at them. "You're right. I'm sweating. Why the hell am I sweating if I'm so cold? Do you think I'm sick?"

Even if Darien did think Farris was sick, he certainly wasn't going to suggest they go to the hospital. He'd seen how Farris would react to that.

Gesturing toward the bed, he asked, "May I sit?"

"Yes." Blinking, Farris seemed surprised that Darien would ask permission before he did it.

Darien picked up the blade off the cover then set it on the nightstand. He turned to look at Farris who stared at him with just a hint of panic in his eyes. Yet Darien saw a little flicker of interest when Farris realized Darien was naked.

"Sorry. It's too fucking hot in this place for me to wear clothes to bed." Darien smiled. "I can put something on if you want."

"It's fine. I don't care what you wear." Farris might have tried to pretend to be casual about Darien's nakedness, but Darien watched as Farris followed the trail of hair leading down Darien's abs to his pubes.

"All right. Here's the thing, sir—"

Farris interrupted, "I guess you could probably call me Farris when we're here. Seems silly to make you call me sir when you're naked in my room. I'm not a Dom or anything like that."

Darien snorted, but wisely chose not to comment on that. "I think you being cold is in your mind. I don't think your body really is cold."

"That's crazy and I'm not crazy. No matter what the fuck my brother says. I went through thirteen years of hell trying to convince them I was sane." Farris' gaze shot over to the far wall. "I finally figured out to say what they wanted to hear. I told them I lied about Tomas being real. That he never existed outside my mind."

A jolt of excitement rushed through Darien at the mention of Tomas. Could it possibly be the man he was searching for? He didn't know how to bring that up, so he decided to broach that subject later.

"I know you're not crazy. Or at least not any crazier than the rest of us. What I think is that your mind is convinced you're freezing. I think it happens when you're stressed." Darien edged an inch or two closer. "I hate asking this of you, but did something happen while you were away? Something that happened when you didn't behave?"

Farris didn't stop staring at the opposite wall, but he stiffened when a thought must have hit him. "My room was so cold. They never turned the heat on, even during the winter. I used to yell at them to get me some fucking blankets, but they just laughed at me. When I argued with them, they would throw cold water on me. I would sit soaked in the middle of the room and they wouldn't let me change. I had to sit there."

Darien bit back his growl of anger. No one deserved to be treated like that. He'd heard there used to be places that did that to their patients, but now they were in the twenty-first century. One would think that modern man had outgrown torturing the less fortunate like that.

He gave himself a mental slap upside the head. All he had to do was go into the other wards of Chicago to see all the terrible things men in power could do to those who had none. It shouldn't shock him that Farris had been treated that badly.

"The more I argued with them or protested anything they did, the more they'd do things like that to me. Bathtubs full of ice and they would submerge me. Hold me under until I thought I'd drown." Farris shivered and Darien clenched his hands to keep from wrapping his arms around the man.

"I think those events have caused a short circuit in your brain. Not like insanity or anything like that. You were furious at your brother earlier today, weren't you?"

Farris nodded as he shot a quick glance over at Darien before returning to studying the other side of the room.

"Well, see when you were angry at the asylum, they'd douse you in cold water or stuff you in an ice bath."

"I haven't been in that shithole for five years," Farris pointed out.

Darien nodded. "I realize that, but you're still caught up in the responses you were taught. Anger equals cold. So your mind thinks you should be freezing when you get angry."

Farris took a deep breath and Darien waited to hear him yell at him for saying such stupid shit, but Farris exhaled slowly. His shivering calmed a little as his grip on the blankets eased.

Darien tried not to stare at the expanse of pale skin exposed while the covers slipped. Farris might be slender, but there was some muscle on the man and his pink nipples stood out against his skin. There was a scattering of red hair on his chest leading down to his stomach. Darien licked his lips before looking away. He couldn't ogle his boss, not when the man was struggling against his own demons.

"You could be right," Farris admitted. "But how do I fix it?"

"That I'm not completely sure of." Darien shrugged. "I wish I had an answer."

He almost fell off the bed when Farris' hand came to rest on his arm. He stared down at it for a moment then covered it with his. He swallowed hard before he looked up. Farris watched him with narrowed eyes like he was trying to read his mind. Just as Darien was about to pull away, Farris leaned forward and pressed a kiss to Darien's lips.

Motionless, Darien didn't break the kiss, but he didn't take it any deeper either. This wasn't something he'd planned and he wasn't about to push Farris for anything more. Of course, he was human and his boss was rather gorgeous. Red curls and pale skin with icy blue eyes. Sure, he'd been more focused on Farris' emotional and mental issues, but he wasn't blind and he'd always been attracted to the man.

His cock hardened as Farris lapped at his mouth, begging for entrance instead of demanding it like Darien expected him to. Darien eased back slightly, leaving a few inches between them. He met Farris' gaze, noticing that for the first time his eyes weren't cold.

"Are you sure about this?" he had to ask. He didn't want to deal with Farris' regrets in the morning.

Chapter Three

Farris bit his bottom lip while he considered Darien's question. Was he sure about this? He hadn't been interested in sex with anyone for a very long time. So much of his time and attention had been centered on taking his brother down that he never noticed other people around him.

It might have only been a day since he'd met Darien, yet his body had accepted him into his personal space. Usually he'd be yelling at him to stay away from him. He stared at Darien who watched him closely.

Looking over the man, Farris noticed that his original thoughts about Darien were true. He was all muscle, big and wide. His skin held a little tan and there was a smattering of dark hair on his chest. Farris let his gaze drop to Darien's groin where his cock rose hard and solid from its nest of tight curls. There were a few scars marring Darien's skin, but nothing like the ones that tore across Farris'.

After taking a deep breath, he looked back up to meet Darien's green eyes.

Am I sure about this?

He didn't know if he trusted Darien completely, but he discovered he didn't care. Farris was amazed to find he wanted to feel a warm body next to him, pressing him into the mattress while filling him.

"Yes," he blurted out just as Darien started to look like he was thinking about pulling away.

His consent seemed to be the only thing Darien had been waiting for. Darien reached out slowly, but didn't hesitate when he wrapped his arms around Farris to pull him close. Frustrated at the covers keeping them apart, Farris yanked them to the side, needing to feel all of Darien's skin against his.

The instant their naked bodies came together, Farris groaned, adoring the heat because, even if Darien was right and the cold was all in his mind, Farris still needed the warmth. He wound his arms and legs around Darien like an octopus, doing his best to bring as much flesh into contact as possible. Then their erections brushed against each other and he shuddered.

"Do you have any supplies?" Darien whispered in his ear.

Farris stopped moving for a second as he thought before shaking his head. "No. I haven't."

Darien placed his finger on Farris' lips to keep him from continuing. "I understand. Why don't you climb back under those blankets while I go get some?"

He didn't want Darien to leave, irrationally afraid that the man would disappear if he left the room. Farris grasped that his fear came from what had happened to Tomas all those years ago, but there was a reason why it was called irrational, just like his inability to get warm no matter how high the temperature was in the apartment. He fought the urge to cling.

Placing his hand on Farris' face, Darien lifted so they were staring at each other. "I'll be right back, Farris. I won't disappear and no one's going to take me away from you."

How had he known what Farris was worried about? Farris nodded, letting just a bit of his walls come down to hand some trust over to Darien. He watched as Darien left the room before curling up under the blankets. While lying there, he wondered if maybe there were too many covers on the bed. He quickly stripped three of them off, letting them fall to the floor.

When Darien entered the second time, Farris was sprawled out, head on the pillow and stroking himself. Darien set the rubber down before joining Farris on the bed. He popped open the bottle of lube then squirted some on his fingers. He got the bottle closed, and Farris took it from him to let it fall to the mattress.

Darien tucked a pillow under Farris' hips then trailed his fingers down over Farris' balls to circle his hole. Farris inhaled as he did his best to spread his thighs farther apart. He wanted Darien to have as much access as he could.

"Hmm…how long has it been?" Darien eased just the tip of one finger into him.

Farris clenched around the invading digit, not really eager to share the fact that he hadn't had sex in years. "At least fifteen."

"Fifteen?" Darien paused and Farris could almost see him adding and subtracting years in his mind. "You had sex while you were in the hospital?"

"I wouldn't really call it sex." He didn't want to talk about it.

Darien reared back so he could look at Farris. "You weren't raped, were you?"

As much as he didn't want to discuss his last sexual encounter, he also didn't want Darien to pity him more than he already did. He shook his head. "No. It wasn't rape. Just wasn't very fun."

He arched his back, doing his best to bring more of Darien in. Darien frowned, but must have chosen not to comment on that, which was good because Farris really didn't want to take a trip down memory lane. Not when all of his memories centered around that pit of hell he'd been held captive in.

Darien pushed two fingers in and Farris let his head fall back at the fullness. His body resisted it for a minute, but Farris breathed deep, forcing himself to relax so Darien could stretch him. He didn't care about the burn or the slight pain, knowing it would go away eventually. All he wanted was more and deeper.

"Holy fuck!" Farris almost shot out of the bed when Darien nailed his gland for the first time. His own cock stiffened even more, aching with the need to come.

"Just a little more," Darien murmured. "I don't want to hurt you."

Farris shook his head then scrambled to find the condom. "No. I want you inside me. I can deal with a little pain." *Not like I haven't been doing that all my life.*

"All right." Darien ripped open the package to reveal the rubber.

Watching Darien roll the latex over his cock, Farris couldn't help but reach out to pump Darien's hard-on once. Darien grabbed his hand to stop him. He glanced up to see the man shaking his head.

"Don't. I won't last long if you keep touching and looking at me like that." Darien poured more lube on his cock then coated it before positioning himself at Farris' opening. He put Farris' legs over his arms then, meeting his gaze, Darien pushed in.

Closing his eyes, Farris pushed back, taking Darien in one long shove. He wouldn't let Darien stop until he was buried as far inside as he could go. Once their bodies accepted each other's touch, their movements halted for a moment as Farris opened his eyes to stare up at Darien.

Darien let go of his legs then reached out to take Farris' left hand in his. He lifted his wrist to his mouth before placing a kiss at the start of the scar that tore up Farris' arm. Farris blinked away tears he'd never thought he'd ever shed again.

"Are you okay?" Darien's soft question caught him off guard, but Farris nodded.

Again not wanting to talk about it, he clenched his muscles to massage the length of Darien's cock. Darien entwined their fingers together then pinned them to the mattress before he started moving.

Farris moved with him, undulating and tightening. He did everything he could think of to bring Darien to the edge of his climax. After each stroke in, Darien hit Farris' gland with each pull out. Soon their movements no longer matched as they both needed to come.

"Jesus, Farris!" Darien shouted as he climaxed, flooding the condom with his seed.

Farris whimpered as his own orgasm hit him and strings of pearly cum spilled out of his cock to coat his stomach.

Darien continued to ride him, drawing out all the pleasure he could. Farris allowed it to wash over and break down some more of his walls. It was hard to continue to hate the world and the people in it when he had such joy rushing through him. Exhaling loudly, Farris sank back into the mattress as all of his tension drained from him.

He grunted as Darien collapsed on top of him. Farris encircled Darien's heaving shoulders then smoothed his hands up and down the man's back, doing his best to help calm Darien.

Farris lost track of time as they held each other until their breathing synchronized and their racing hearts evened out. Darien pulled out of his embrace before climbing out of the bed to take care of the condom.

When Darien came to clean Farris off, he couldn't take it. He grabbed the cloth from Darien to do it himself. "I've got this."

"But—" Darien started to protest and Farris shook his head.

"I spent thirteen years being washed by other people. I'm perfectly capable of doing it myself." Farris got it over with as fast as possible then tossed the washcloth in the direction of the door. He shivered once before diving back under the blankets.

Darien hesitated, but when Farris lifted up the covers, he rejoined him. Lying back, Farris stared up at the ceiling, wondering if he'd be able to get used to having someone share his bed again. Tomas was the last man he'd welcomed to it.

He jerked when Darien caressed his cheek. "Farris, who was Tomas?"

Fuck! Did I really say his name aloud? "I don't know a Tomas."

A look of disappointment crossed Darien's face then an expression of determination. "You said that every time you mentioned Tomas being a real person, the staff at the hospital would discipline you."

"Why do you want to know?" Farris might have been willing to share his body with Darien, but he wasn't entirely sure he trusted the man with the secret held so close to his heart.

"A dear friend of mine has a cousin named Tomas, and this friend is interested to know what happened to his cousin." Darien didn't drop his gaze, just kept staring at Farris.

"He was murdered," Farris muttered. "My bastard of a brother murdered him eighteen years ago, then wiped out any proof the man existed."

Darien nodded. "Do you have a picture of your Tomas?"

Farris tensed, all happiness gained from making love with Darien disappearing beneath memories. After rolling out of bed, he paced the room, waving his hands in the air while he argued with himself.

"You can't risk it. What happens if he's a spy sent by your brother to find out what you're doing? What if you tell him and he tells Ralph? You'll end up dead—or worse, he'll send you back to the asylum."

He continued muttering to himself. Hands landed on his shoulders and he froze, wondering what was going to happen. Darien nuzzled his temple as he pulled him back against his chest.

"I won't let anything happen to you, Farris. You can trust me."

Farris shrugged as he laughed. "Seriously? You're telling me to trust you when I don't know you? After everything that has happened in my life, you expect me to give you all my secrets and memories without worrying you'll use them against me?"

"No, I don't expect you tell me all your secrets. I just want to know about Tomas. Whatever else you have hidden is yours to keep. My friend and I are trying to figure out what happened to him and where he might be." Darien rubbed his hands over Farris' trembling arms. "Why don't you come back to bed? You really are cold now."

"It's the fear in my soul manifesting," Farris informed him, but he let Darien lead him over.

After crawling back under the covers, he wrapped his arms around a pillow, holding it close to his chest while he studied Darien. "Why should I trust you?"

"Like I said, I don't want to know anything about what else you have going on, Farris. I'm only interested in Tomas."

A sudden thought hit him. "Is that the reason why you fucked me?"

Darien grimaced at Farris' rather crude question. "No. I would've fucked you, no matter what. I wanted you from the moment I saw you."

Farris raised an eyebrow. "Crazy anti-social men push your buttons, Shaunessy?"

"I don't know if any other crazy person would, but you do, O'Laughlin, and once I get some more rubbers, I'll prove it to you." Darien clasped Farris' hands in his. "Please tell me about Tomas, Farris. I know you haven't been able to tell anyone, so let me carry the burden with you."

Farris stared at their hands for a second before making a decision. It didn't matter if Darien turned him into his brother. His mission was almost complete. He simply needed to find a way to get the information out to the world. Once that happened, his brother's power would be destroyed and Farris would have his revenge.

"I met Tomas when I was nineteen. I managed to keep our relationship a secret from my family. Not because I was ashamed of Tomas, even though he was from Third Ward and my parents would've freaked at the thought of the O'Laughlin heir seeing a Hispanic from one of the poorer wards." Farris shook his head. "I didn't care, though I will admit I never went to visit him at his place. I couldn't risk getting kidnapped or something then held for ransom. It could've been a whole year's worth of salary for some of the people in that area."

Darien didn't say anything, so Farris decided to keep going. "I was being groomed to take over my father's place as head of the family. It's a tradition that I would become head of the gang when I turned twenty-one. Well, days before I reached majority, my brother sprung his trap. He killed Tomas then told me about it."

He relived the overwhelming pain and rage when his brother had told him what he'd done. Farris had gone after his brother, swearing to kill him, but Ralph's bodyguards had stopped him. Then when Farris had gone to their father with it, Ralph had exposed his brilliant plan. He'd shown proof that Tomas didn't exist, had never existed, and that Farris was raving about an invisible person.

Maybe his father had been in on the plan. Maybe his father hadn't wanted a fag running the business. That thought had been in the back of Farris' mind for all his time away, but his father had died before Farris got out and could ask.

"I did everything I could to prove Tomas was real and that Ralph had killed him, but no one believed me. More than likely, my father didn't want to believe me," Farris admitted. "He consented to having me committed and Ralph sent me to Wisconsin before I even had time to counter what he'd done. I was locked up for thirteen years, beaten and tortured until I finally told them what they wanted. That Tomas wasn't real and it was best that Ralph took over the family."

Darien lifted his hands to his mouth then kissed his knuckles. "I'm sorry."

Farris shrugged. "I cared about him. I have no idea if I would've stayed with him forever or not. We weren't from the same worlds. Now I'll never know because he's dead. I need to destroy my brother and get revenge."

"It's nice that you want revenge for what he did to Tomas."

His forehead wrinkled in confusion, Farris looked at Darien. "Tomas? Sure, I'd like to teach Ralph a lesson about killing people who belong to me, but I'd just beat the shit out of him if that was the only reason. I'm going to destroy everything Ralph holds dear because he took my life away from me."

Darien sighed and it sounded rather resigned. "I should've known it wasn't all about Tomas."

"I'm not a saint, but I'm willing to admit that some of it *is* for Tomas. The bastard killed him."

"Wait. Umm...I'm not entirely sure Tomas is dead." Darien pursed his lips while Farris stared at him, shocked by the revelation.

Farris shook his head. "Not dead? How would you know that? Ralph erased everything pertaining to Tomas."

"I saw him about six years ago here in Chicago. The good news is he looked okay."

"What was the bad news?" Farris narrowed his eyes because he just knew he wasn't going to like it.

Darien's eyes skittered away from his gaze then back. "He was with slavers."

Farris shot up in bed, letting the blankets pool around his waist. "Ralph fucking sold him to slavers? The bastard deserves to have his heart cut out with a spoon," he snarled. "Do you know where he is now?"

"No. My friend and I have looked all over the city, but it's kind of hard to move between the wards if you don't have papers or a reason to be there. For all intents and purposes, he's gone now. We can't find him anywhere." Darien frowned down at Farris' scar. "I just hope he's still alive now. It's been a lot of years since he disappeared again. We're holding out hope that he's survived being a slave somehow."

Farris tugged his hands away from Darien's to scrub them over his face. Should he tell Darien all of the truth? Would having access to all that information help them find Tomas? If the man was still alive, Farris did want to find him. It would be revenge on his brother, but also remove some of the guilt Farris felt for having involved Tomas in his family.

He watched Darien while he ran all of his thoughts through his head. Maybe giving all of it to Darien would work. Darien seemed like the kind of guy who might have connections who could get what Farris had to the right people. Farris wasn't completely sure what he had, though he knew enough to know it could take his brother down.

"Tomas' cousin wants to find him, and I've been helping him. We knew that his last lover was an O'Laughlin, so I decided to get a job with your family, hoping to find some kind of information out about him." Darien smiled. "I have to admit, I never dreamed you were the lover."

"Not many people remember me when I was younger. They only see the insane O'Laughlin and they pat Ralph on the back for finding a job for me. So you really didn't sleep with me just to get the past out of me?"

Darien shook his head. "No. If I thought you would've said yes, I would've approached you sooner, even if I lost my job for sleeping with you."

"Sex over a job? Not very wise." Farris winked.

"Maybe not, but it's not like I couldn't find a job somewhere else." Darien urged Farris to lie back in his arms. "Thank you for telling me all of that, Farris. It does help a little bit."

Farris took a deep breath and a leap of faith. "If I show you something else, do you promise not to use it against me?"

He realized it was a stupid question. He'd already talked about Tomas, and if Darien was that kind of guy, he would be calling Ralph the moment Farris fell asleep. Darien smoothed his hand over Farris' head.

"I won't use anything you say to me against you. I have no interest in ever talking to your brother or any other member of the O'Laughlins, except for you." Darien rubbed his nose against Farris' and Farris had to fight the urge to shove the man off the bed.

"Personal space, man." Farris pushed Darien a few inches away instead.

Darien chuckled and Farris smiled. For the first time in a while, he didn't feel cold, and he felt connected to what was going on around him, even if it was only in his bedroom.

"All right. I have something else to show you." He made a decision, and realized he really was going to be okay, because he had his escape plan and it was ready to be put into effect whenever he needed to do so. So if Darien turned out to be a liar, then Farris could still get the hell out of Chicago before his brother found out.

He climbed out of bed then went to the dresser to pull a small box out of a drawer.

Chapter Four

Darien watched Farris return to their bed, holding something. He took what Farris handed him. It was a small black jewelry box and when he opened it, he saw two cufflinks sparkling up at him.

"Cufflinks?" Looking up, he realized Farris had gone to his closet to pull a laptop out from a hidden hole in the back wall. "Why do I think that's not registered?"

The smile Farris shot him could only be described as wolfish. "What makes you think that?"

"I don't know. What do cufflinks and a laptop have to do with what you want to show me?" He wasn't sure if he should be worried or not.

Farris sat cross-legged on the bed, turning the laptop on while reaching for the box. "These aren't just cufflinks."

As Darien watched, Farris removed the diamond from the first link then twisted the setting until it shifted into a flash drive. Once the computer was up and running, Farris slid the drive into the port and clicked on the icon. He typed in a password before clicking on a file.

Farris handed it over to Darien then leaned back against the headboard to see how Darien reacted. As he scrolled through the numbers and names, excitement began to grow in Darien's soul.

"Is this real?" He glanced up to meet Farris' gaze.

"Yes. I've been working for five years to gather as much information as I could to bring Ralph down. I want to destroy the only thing he loves, which is the O'Laughlin family business. If it's shattered, he has nothing." Farris was practically rubbing his hands together and gloating.

Darien touched his arm. "But that means you have nothing as well. You might just be a collector, but you are part of the family."

Farris laughed. "I've been making sure I have an escape plan for this very occasion. Don't worry about me, Darien. I'll be fine when this goes down."

After pointing at the other cufflink in the box, he asked, "Are both of them flash drives?"

"Yes. The files and spreadsheets on both those drives can stop the Immigration Bill from being passed, and they will bring the Feds into the city. You know they've been salivating to get into Chicago and clean it up."

That wasn't a well-kept secret. The Feds did everything they could to get their own agents into the city to spy on the city council and the gangs. So far it hadn't been successful, but who knew it would only take one revenge-minded family member to take the whole house of cards down?

"You do understand what you have here, right?" He gestured toward the screen.

Farris rolled his eyes. "I'm not stupid, Darien. Of course I know what I have. I made sure I had the most incriminating numbers, names and photographs I could get. Just taking Ralph down won't hurt him that badly, but taking the entire organization down? That will hurt all of them who didn't say a word when my brother locked me away."

He was rubbing his wrist again, and Darien understood that it was going to take time to prove to Farris that things were better. His heart skipped a beat when Farris smiled at him and there wasn't a hint of rage or blankness in his eyes. For the first time, aside from when they'd had sex, Farris was present with him.

"You do know that this won't take down the entire political structure, but it'll help thousands of people who live in this city," he informed his lover.

Shrugging, Farris said, "That doesn't concern me. I really don't care what happens to them."

Snorting softly, Darien nodded. It wasn't surprising to hear Farris say something like that and Darien got that he was to be the one with a conscience in their relationship. He let that go while he thought about what to do with the bomb Farris had dropped into his lap.

"I can do whatever I want with this?"

Farris pursed his lips then nodded. "I guess so."

"You trust me enough to know that I'll do what needs to be done with it?"

"It no longer matters whether I trust you or not. You know about the laptop, the flash drives and all the stuff I have. If I think you screwed me over, I'll bail and you'll have all that you need while I'm staying warm on a tropical island." Farris secmed rather proud of himself.

Darien accepted that. "All right. I think I know who I can give this to. I need to make a phone call."

Farris climbed out of the bed then headed toward the door and Darien called out, "Where are you going?"

"You make your phone call and I'll take a shower." Farris flapped his hand in Darien's direction. "Do what you have to do."

"Thank you."

His lover disappeared into the hallway, obviously not interested in listening to Darien's conversation. Darien left the room as well to return to his where his phone was. After digging it out, he scrolled through to find Cesar's number. He tapped his name to dial.

"What are you calling me for, Darien? I thought we said we wouldn't get in touch unless it's really important."

"Cesar, I've discovered a way to stop you from having to leave the city and to effect change on the leadership." He dropped his bombshell on his friend, knowing Cesar would be able to decipher his ambiguous comment.

Cesar swore loudly and Darien marveled at the man's creativity. "The fuck you say. How did you come across such treasure?"

"Let's say a friend of Tomas' came back into town and has been looking into things. He's decided to let me do what I want with it." Darien wasn't interested in dragging Farris or his name into it, though Cesar wasn't stupid. He'd figure it out eventually.

"Tomas? Do you know where he is?"

Darien sighed. "No. That isn't the information I got, but I think I might be able to find some more out about what happened to him."

Cesar growled low, frustration evident in his tone. "Good. So you have something you think I need to look at?"

"Yes. But I can't bring it directly to you. I don't want to get someone in trouble any sooner than necessary." Darien really wanted to keep Farris safe.

"Okay. Let me make some calls and see what I can do. The treasure might have to travel a little bit, but it'll get to me without getting anyone in trouble." Cesar hung up without saying goodbye.

Darien tossed his phone on his bed then got dressed. The shower was off and he could hear Farris in his own room when he walked into the living room. Farris wandered in, buttoning one of his sleeves.

He caught the man before he could fasten it. Rolling the cuff up, Darien ran his fingers over the jagged scar. "When did you do this?"

Farris shrugged, feigning nonchalance. "About five years into my enforced hospital stay. Decided I couldn't deal with it all. Took the coward's way out."

"I'm glad you didn't succeed," Darien admitted as he pulled Farris into his arms. "I wouldn't be able to get to know you, and I really want to see how serious you and I can become."

"You think we have a chance to be more than fuck buddies?" Farris rested his cheek on Darien's chest while sliding his arms around Darien's waist.

Darien smiled, but didn't answer. He just kissed the top of Farris' head before squeezing the man tight. They stood like that for a couple of minutes, then Farris broke away to pace.

"Do you really think whoever you called can ensure this information gets to the right people?" Farris pulled the jewelry box out of his pocket. "Or should I look for someone else?"

"No, he's the right person. You do realize there's a resistance group in Chicago? They want to overthrow the city council and gangs." He didn't think Farris was that stupid about what was going on in Chicago.

Farris waved his hand. "Of course there is. My brother doesn't think it exists or that the poor people would dare to go against the gangs. It's the epitome of arrogance for him to believe that there aren't people who want to take away what he has."

Darien's phone rang and he checked the screen while motioning to Farris to be quiet. He answered, "Hello?"

"You're to take the package to Elijah's Drugstore in Second Ward. A man will meet you there." Cesar hung up.

After putting his phone in his pocket, he glanced at Farris. "I need to pick up some medicine from the drugstore."

Farris shrugged. "Fine. I'll wait here for you to get back."

"No. You have to go with me." He knew Farris was going to ask him and he didn't want to tell him. Plausible deniability. That's what he wanted Farris to have.

"Why?"

"The drugstore I use is in Second Ward and you can get us into the ward without any hassle." Darien grabbed his keys before jerking a jacket out of the closet for Farris.

Farris scowled. "So you're using me for my influence?"

"Yes, I am for this. Not for anything else." Darien cupped Farris' pointed chin then kissed him. He took the box from Farris before stuffing it in his pocket.

"How do I know you're not doing all of this just to use me to find Tomas?" Farris asked after the kiss was done. He didn't sound particularly annoyed or worried about what Darien's answer might be.

He chuckled. "Honey, we're using each other for that."

Nodding, Farris walked out of the apartment. Darien patted his pocket to make sure he had the package then followed his lover to the elevator.

"What's so important that we have to go all the way into the outer wards to get it?" Farris frowned.

Darien knew he hated leaving the comfort and protection of First Ward. Once they left the relative safety of the ward, desperate people looking to make easy money could kidnap them. Farris would also be confronted by the poverty his family and the other gangs were causing the residents of Chicago.

The information Farris had given him would be the first step in helping give Chicago a better future and its people a brighter tomorrow. Darien understood that Farris didn't care about any of that idealistic bullshit.

* * * *

"It's a brave thing you're doing, man," his contact said as he took the package from Darien.

Shaking his head, Darien glanced over his shoulder to where Farris stood, arms crossed and a look of annoyance on his face. That expression wasn't for show. If anyone asked why they were at this particular store at this particular moment, Farris could say he had no idea why his driver chose to stop there. His lover would be innocent of this one act of rebellion, and Darien would catch the brunt of the blame.

It was what he wanted since it had been a little push from him that had set them both on this course. Farris would've never chosen this path for revenge. Not originally. No, the man was nothing if not direct, and a knife into his brother's back would've suited him just fine. But his time in the asylum had taught him there were less direct ways to destroy a person, and he was more than happy to allow Darien to start the process in motion.

"It shouldn't be considered brave to help when things go wrong. It should simply be common sense," he muttered.

The delivery guy nodded. "I guess you're right. Well, I'll take this and make sure it gets to where it needs to go."

"Thank you."

Darien didn't stick around to watch the man leave. He took his purchase then walked over to where Farris leaned against the car. Approaching his lover cautiously, Darien stood next to him, so close their bodies touched from shoulder to hip. Farris shifted his weight, letting Darien take some of it.

"Are you done?" Farris didn't look at him, just continued staring at the people walking by them.

"Yes, sir." Darien managed to sound polite, but Farris snorted as if he heard some kind of sarcasm in Darien's voice.

"Fine. Then let's go. My brother wants me to make an appearance at some event tonight with him and the Deputy Mayor," Farris informed Darien. "I would rather shove a fork in my eye, but such is the life of the man I've become."

Darien couldn't stop from reaching out to lay his hand on Farris' arm. They hadn't yet touched in public because a member of the O'Laughlin family would never allow their servants to be so familiar with them. Farris glared down at his hand, then up at his face.

"It's started," Darien murmured softly.

A hint of panic raced across Farris' face, then Darien watched as another more visceral and hate-filled gleam came into Farris' eyes.

"Good. Now I can look at my brother and know that his time is coming to an end," Farris growled and bared his teeth.

Need hit Darien low in the gut, and all he could think about was getting Farris into the back of the car where he could fuck him until the man cried out his name. It wasn't possible here on the busy streets of Chicago, but at some point during the next day or two, he would find an alley to pull into and have his chance at Farris' ass.

Maybe it was wrong of Darien to love a man like Farris O'Laughlin. Even though Farris would forever be known as the man who started the revolution, he hadn't done it out of compassion for those less fortunate than him. Hell, Farris didn't have a clue about those who would be affected by this 'immigration' bill and he didn't care about them either.

From the very beginning of their adventure, all Farris cared about was hurting his brother like he had been hurt. Whether it helped or hurt anyone else, Farris didn't care as long as it furthered his own goals. Maybe that wasn't the kind of man Darien should be thinking of being with all his life, but he was and he couldn't really put a reason to that.

"We'll get you home with enough time to change." He opened the back door then gestured for Farris to enter the car.

As he was climbing in, a thought must have crossed Farris' mind. He touched Darien's hand for a second. "You made sure you won't be implicated in anything? I don't want this coming back on you."

And right there was why Darien was willing to give his heart to Farris. While he might have no interest in people he didn't know, Farris cared deeply about the people he loved, and Darien knew he was top on that list.

Nothing about this had to do with bravery for Farris and Darien accepted that. But Farris' love shined through in his trust that Darien's choice for what to do with the information was the right thing to do.

"Don't worry, Farris. Neither of us are in danger of being discovered," he whispered.

Nodding, Farris got in the back then Darien shut the door. Before he took his place behind the wheel, Darien stared up into the blue sky.

"God speed," he said, sending up a prayer that whatever they set in play wouldn't end up getting anyone killed. "Please keep Tomas safe until we can find him."

LOVE DON'T DIE

Jambrea Jo Jones

Dedication

I'm so happy to be included with this wonderful bunch of ladies. I have such fun every year and it just keeps getting better and better.

Chapter One

Moran Schultz accepted the package being handed to him and put it in his pants pocket. It was dangerous, but he wasn't scared. It had to be done if he ever wanted a real chance to be with Dutch Luciano. Right now it wasn't safe for them to be together. And if what had been promised was enclosed, it would blow things wide open. In *his* lifetime. He had been losing hope. The gangs had such a tight clutch on Chicago.

"It's a brave thing you're doing, man."

Not many would stand up to the gangs. There were pockets of resistance and they grew stronger every day, but with this vital information, their fighting might not all be for nothing. He didn't know exactly what it was, but when Cesar said it was big, people believed the head of the resistance and did whatever they could to help.

"It shouldn't be considered brave to help when things go wrong. It should simply be common sense," Darien Shaunessy muttered.

Moran nodded. "I guess you're right. Well, I'll take this and make sure it gets to where it needs to go."

"Thank you."

There was no need for his contact to thank him. Moran was doing the job his brother had requested of him. And he wanted to be free from the gangs just as much as any other low end worker in the grid.

He watched Darien walk out of the store and if he wasn't mistaken he was headed to Farris O'Laughlin. The crazy brother. Fuck. He needed to get out of there. Was this a set up? Cesar wouldn't lead him to a set up. He was too careful. Moran continued to watch them and no enforcers charged the building.

One of the biggest families was involved? He wasn't going to ask any questions—hell, he should probably forget what he'd just seen. It wasn't his job. Darien did seem a bit cozy with the brother. He slowly backed away and edged out of the back door. The drugstore was a safe zone in Second Ward. His brother's people ran it, but it never hurt to be as safe as he could. He wasn't as important as his brother, but that didn't mean people wouldn't use him to get to the head of Second Ward's resistance.

"Hey there. Watch it."

Moran closed his eyes. That voice. He knew that voice and it shouldn't be here in this ward. Fucking Dutch Luciano. The guy used to be part of the gangs, but was now a member of the resistance. The last time they'd gotten caught together one of the enforcers had run Dutch's tag and found he wasn't where he belonged. Moran had had to watch while his very soul had been ripped out punch by punch. He'd gotten off easy because he was supposed to be there. They'd left Dutch in a puddle of blood at his feet. Moran couldn't get that picture out of his head. Dutch's eyes closed, his body motionless. Moran had thought he was dead. There wasn't anything he'd been able to do as the enforcers had dragged Dutch off. It had taken two weeks to find out that his lover hadn't died, and he'd vowed right then to cut off all communications. His heart ached at the thought of that happening again. He had to get Dutch out of there. The drugstore might be a safe zone, but the thugs still patrolled.

He turned. "Dutch—what the fuck, man? You shouldn't be here," Moran whispered. He couldn't bring himself to look Dutch in the eyes.

It wasn't that a lot of people knew Dutch was resistance, but the man shouldn't be there. If he got caught he could be roughed up or even killed. It wouldn't be a first offense for Dutch. And if the gangs found him, he would wind up dead.

"I talked to Frankie and he said you were here on a pick-up. It was important. I wanted to make sure you got it okay." Dutch shrugged his broad shoulders.

"You send a flunky. It's too dangerous for you here. We've talked about this." Moran shoved his hands in his pockets and clutched at the flash drive.

"No, you've talked about this, but never listen." Dutch reached out to him, but Moran moved away.

"It's over." Moran didn't sound very convincing and he knew it. *Damn it.*

"No, it isn't. So you can stop sending someone else to our meets. I miss you."

Dutch's voice was like a caress to Moran's ears, but he couldn't be weak.

"You think I don't miss you too? We can't be together. It's going to get you killed." Moran could handle being apart as long as he knew Dutch was alive.

"So I die a happy man." There was a smile in that tone, but Moran wasn't going to look up to see.

"Don't fucking joke about that." Moran clenched his teeth. He would die if Dutch was no longer on this Earth.

"Who's joking?"

"Go home, Dutch."

"You get it?" Dutch was trying to change the subject.

It was a skill of his, but Moran wasn't going to let it slide. They had to get Dutch back to Zero. He looked around to see if anyone was paying attention to them, but so far they were in the clear. He had to act fast. Maybe if he started walking toward Zero Dutch would follow and not put up too much of a fuss.

"I did, but this doesn't concern Zero Ward. It's going to Third and so on. So go home and if Frankie needs to get you information someone will be in touch. Now sneak out like you got in before someone sounds the alarm. You're face isn't anonymous here. Didn't you learn anything from last month? Fuck. Leave."

"Come with me." Dutch reached out a hand.

"I can't right now. I've got to wait for the next contact point and get this out of my hands."

"I'll wait with you."

God, he wanted that so very much, but he couldn't be selfish.

"I can't watch it happen again, Dutch. You can't keep doing this to me—" His voice broke on the last word and he flashed back to that night.

"They didn't kill me, Morrie. Come on. Look at me."

Moran didn't know if he could. He was staring at a button on Dutch's coat. He'd give in if he looked into Dutch's green eyes.

"Don't you understand this is hard?" He clenched his fist inside his pants because he was going to reach out for Dutch.

"Then stop resisting us. Please, baby. Let's go to your place. We'll talk."

"You need to find someone in your own ward." God, it hurt Moran to even think that let alone say it.

"I'm not leaving until you can look at me and tell me you don't love me."

Dutch held his breath and waited for those dark brown eyes to focus on his face. He knew with every fiber of his being that Morrie loved him. He just had to convince him it was worth it. Hell, he'd give up his pocket of resistance if he could get relocated to Second Ward, but that shit was hard to do. He could fake the paperwork, but finding someone good enough to make the papers wasn't easy. Most of them worked for the gangs and would know his face. He was an exile. When it had been found out he liked men he'd been left for dead outside of Zero Ward and told not to leave — if he survived.

Morrie was worth every second of Dutch's time. When they'd first met the lust had been there, but after years of dealing with Morrie as a go between, they'd gotten to know each other and lust had turned to love — on both their parts — and Dutch wasn't going to let Morrie back out.

"You know I can't do that." Morrie turned away from him.

This wasn't working out how he wanted it to. He figured he'd give Morrie some time apart and his lover would realize they belonged together despite the odds.

"Take me home, Morrie. You know Cesar won't give you instructions until tomorrow because he'll want to make sure there is no heat. I talked to Frankie. This is too important to rush. We're being careful."

"How careful is it for one of the leaders of the resistance, an ex-gang member, to be in the wrong section?"

"You could keep your voice down. Most people don't know who I am."

"They have eyes, Dutch. There are posters all around town. If the wrong person sees you—"

"That's why I said take me home."

"Fuck."

Finally Morrie looked up at him. His lover was so sad. Dutch was going to put an end to this. He grabbed Morrie's hand and headed to his lover's apartment. It was close to the drugstore so they didn't have far to go. This would stop. They loved each other and he wasn't going to let the gangs keep him from being happy. He'd waited too long to find the person who completed him. Morrie was that man and Dutch wasn't giving him up without a fight, even if he was fighting Morrie to keep them together.

"This is a really fucking bad idea." Morrie tugged his hand away, but he kept walking.

Good. He'd remind his lover just how great it was between them. It had been too long. He let himself fall back a bit so he could watch Morrie walk. God, he loved that ass and wanted it naked in front of him.

It's not just about sex. Focus.

Everything looked the same along this row of condos. They made it inside the nondescript building and up to Morrie's place. Dutch stepped to the middle of the room—walking away from Morrie, letting him get his thoughts together. Nothing had changed in the month they'd been apart. He didn't know why he'd thought it would. Maybe because his life had changed that day. He'd been broken and Morrie hadn't been there to fix it. He should have been smarter that day — not let as much time pass before he had someone contact Frankie to tell him he was okay. Morrie's brother didn't fully approve of the relationship, but he wasn't going to keep them apart.

"You need to go home, Dutch." Morrie was against the door, his head tilted back and he was looking at the ceiling.

It might not be about sex, but they needed some sort of connection. Morrie was still pushing him away.

He took off his jacket and laid it across a chair along with his holster and gun. His other clothes could wait. For now he just wanted Morrie in his arms. He walked closer and pulled Morrie away from the door and into his embrace. Morrie struggled for a bit before going completely loose. A moment later his arms circled around Dutch, clinging to him. This is where he belonged, with Morrie in his arms. Morrie's body was shaking.

"Shhh. It's okay. I'm here." He ran his hands up and down Morrie's back. He hated seeing his lover like this. And it was his fault. He knew that, but he *was* here and it could be fixed.

"God, Dutch. You coulda died."

They should have done this weeks ago, but he hadn't wanted to rush things. He should have known better, but he never knew what other obstacles the gangs would throw out there. They'd started talking about this great reform, but Dutch called bullshit. Something big was about to go down and they were hedging their bets. Whatever Morrie had his hands on was going to hopefully stop what the gangs had planned, but right now he didn't care about any of that. He needed to make things right with Morrie.

"But I didn't. We have to be more careful until we can topple—"

"Don't say it."

"We aren't bugged here." They were all overly cautious when it came to listening devices. Most of the resistance had their places swept for bugs religiously.

"Doesn't matter, we need to be careful." Morrie sniffled and moved out of Dutch's arms.

Morrie took the warmth with him. Dutch was so cold, inside and out. He was lost without Morrie and the last month had reinforced that fact to him. They couldn't keep living apart. He wanted to wake up every morning with Morrie in his arms.

"Morrie, let me in."

"I—fuck—I can't. You shouldn't be here." Morrie ran a hand down his face.

Dutch could tell his lover was conflicted, and he hated putting him in this position, but he was going to be selfish. Fuck the gangs. Fuck the resistance.

"I'm not leaving until we have this out."

"I don't love you." Morrie had that blank look on his face, the one he'd used when they'd first met. The one meant to keep people out.

Those words wrecked Dutch. This couldn't be happening. He knew Morrie was afraid, but to go to such lengths to keep them apart? It wasn't like him. Maybe he shouldn't have forced the issue, but he couldn't lose his heart this way.

"I'm not your parents, Mor. I'm not going anywhere. They won't kill me."

"You can't promise that. And I believe you said you would leave if I could tell you I didn't love you. So go." Morrie crossed his arms over his chest, blank look still in place. He couldn't stand it.

"You don't mean it."

"Go."

Morrie had moved away, his back against the wall with nowhere to run. Dutch was going to take advantage of that.

"I'm still here. Look at me. Really look at me. I know what happened was bad, but I'm not a scared twenty-year-old in the wrong place at the wrong time. I can take care of myself."

"The gangs can kill who they want, when they want. My parents may have been young, but they could take care of themselves too. But what happened? They were gunned down outside of a restaurant because the owner owed some money. Collateral damage. Frankie was given a bit of money and that was it. They were gone. You? You almost taunt them saying—'come on, fuckin' kill me'. We're done."

Maybe he should have lured Morrie to his side of the line for this confrontation.

"I'm not taunting anyone."

"Then why are you in a ward you don't belong in? You're pushing it."

"I'm here because the man I love is here and he won't come to me."

Chapter Two

Moran was breaking on the inside, but he couldn't let it show. His love might not die, but he'd be damned if his lover would. He would end this now. Saying he didn't love Dutch had hurt, but not as much as watching him die would.

He needed to get Dutch home. He'd call in Frankie if he had to. His brother would understand and help him. All they had was each other and that was the way it was going to be from here on out. He'd help the resistance when his brother asked him, but other than that, he'd toe the line and work. Keep his mind on stupid stuff that didn't matter.

Dutch moved closer, but there was nowhere for Moran to go. He was literally backed against a wall. He couldn't let Dutch sway him with his words, but if Dutch touched him again, he might not be able to resist. It had been too long, and the last time they'd been together he hadn't been able to comfort Dutch when he was hurt…and now he was here — whole.

"You said you'd leave." Moran wasn't above begging. It might give away his true feelings, but he wasn't fooling Dutch anyway. They knew each other too well.

"I lied." Dutch stalked closer and pressed their bodies together.

Moran wasn't expecting the hard crush of lips on lips. Dutch ground their mouths together. It was too much. He wiggled his arms between them — he was going to push Dutch away, but instead clutched at his shirt. How was he expected to deny the passion between the two of them? It had been there since the first time they'd met.

He groaned and relaxed his body, softening his lips and opening his mouth, letting Dutch inside. This was what he'd been avoiding. Dutch was addictive. Moran would always want him — death wouldn't change that. Moran felt the tears streaming down his face. God. Dutch could have died. That was the part he couldn't get over. Moran wrapped his arms around Dutch and squeezed, grounding himself in his lover's presence. He ripped at the shirt. He needed to feel skin. Moran tugged the silky shirt out of the back of Dutch's pants. He should have unbuttoned it, but that would take too much time.

Dutch didn't stop the brutal assault on his mouth. He ripped the front of his shirt, buttons pinging around the room. Moran smiled against Dutch's lips. He let go so Dutch could pull his shirt off and focused on ridding himself of his own top, tearing the front so he didn't have to move away. Moran sank his teeth into Dutch's bottom lip, tugging on it, then he licked the inside of Dutch's mouth. Dutch groaned. They had skin contact now. All that delicious hair on Dutch's body scraping his skin. He'd be all red by the time they were finished.

Finally he broke the kiss, both of them panting.

"Bedroom." They needed to finish undressing so he could touch every part of Dutch's body.

"No."

"Dutch." He was whining now and didn't care. He wanted Dutch stretched out in front of him.

"Here. Now." Dutch unbuckled his belt, never taking his eyes off Moran.

Fuck that was hot. Moran unbuttoned his pants and shoved them down, underwear and all. Dutch wasn't wearing underwear. He had on a jockstrap. Moran fell to his knees, his pants still around his ankles because he'd forgotten to take off his shoes first. He didn't care. Moran crawled toward Dutch and moved around him until that beautiful ass framed by the jock was in his face. He pushed until Dutch braced himself against the wall. Moran squeezed the cheeks and pulled them apart. Dutch spread his legs, giving Moran more room.

He licked his thumb and ran it over the puckered hole. It wasn't enough. He scooted in closer and buried his face in that wonderful ass. He started slow, nuzzling in, the tip of his tongue brushing the entrance. He used more force and licked at the hole, wiggling his tongue inside, loosening it up. He wanted more than his tongue up that ass, but there was no lube where they were at. He really wished they were in the bedroom for this.

Moran added a finger to the action, searching for the gland that would make Dutch soar.

"Fuck. More."

There it was, he added another finger, still licking the hole. His own cock throbbed, but he couldn't stroke it and keep doing what he was doing.

The choice was taken away from him when Dutch moved out of reach and turned around. His dick peeked through the top of his jock. Moran's mouth watered, he could taste it. Dutch was flattened against the wall, looking down at him. Moran crawled toward him and stretched enough so he could lick the top of that beautiful rod, sucking on the tip. Dutch grasped his hair, not pulling, but steadying himself.

"Morrie. Please."

He tugged at the jock, easing it down Dutch's legs. Moran cupped Dutch's balls and took his shaft down his throat then swallowed. Dutch whimpered. Moran was in control right now and he wasn't going to give it up. He let go of his lover's testicles so he could grasp his hips, giving him a better angle to suck and lick. He didn't know if he wanted Dutch to come now or wait until he was inside. Fuck. He couldn't think clearly and there was so much he wanted to do.

Dutch grabbed his head, making him stop. Moran whimpered, but kept licking. If he couldn't move his head, he would take advantage of the fact that Dutch's cock was still in his mouth.

"Stop. I'm close. Please."

He couldn't resist humming as he released the lovely dick from his mouth. Moran sat back on his haunches and looked up at Dutch. His lover had his head thrown back against the wall with his eyes closed.

"Bedroom?" Moran had to ask again. The lube was in there and he was ready to sink inside Dutch's warm body.

It took Dutch a couple of seconds to realize Morrie had asked a question. His brain was mush, but he didn't expect anything less when with Morrie. His lover was a force to be reckoned with.

He shook his head. No way was he moving. Morrie might be with him right now, but Dutch didn't know if he'd change his mind, and he wasn't going to chance it.

Dutch sucked on two of his fingers and reached behind him, opening himself up.

"Get your cock wet," he demanded of Morrie.

Good thing he was already loose from when Morrie had been playing with his ass. God, he thought he was going to come right then. He loved being rimmed and it was something Morrie enjoyed as well. Thank God. And the feel of Morrie's prickly beard against his skin sent him into overdrive. He loved it when his lover scraped his body using his cheek—the sensation was wonderful. But right now, he wanted that fat cock so far up his ass he could taste it.

He was as stretched as he was going to get. He spit on his palm before kneeling down, straddling Morrie's lap. He wrapped his hand around Morrie's dick, slicking it up a bit more before he lowered himself down on it.

"Dutch!"

The burn was good—fuck he'd missed this. He didn't rush it and once he was fully seated he took a moment to wrap his arms around Morrie and just savor this second in time. Morrie copied the embrace and they clutched at each other.

"Mor, baby, I gotta—"

"Move. Fuck yes."

The slap of skin against skin echoed in the room. It was going to be fast because he could feel his orgasm racing through is body. Dutch rocked faster and faster. Morrie thrust up, his hands braced against the floor. Dutch loved watching his lover come.

"Dutch! Dutch. Fuck. Now, now!" Morrie gave one more thrust and he was coming.

Heat filled Dutch's ass and that was all it took. He only needed his lover's cock in him to bring him to release. His body twitched and Morrie had a hold of his cock, squeezing out the last bits of his come. Dutch clutched his ass, tightening around Morrie's dick, trying to keep him inside as long as he could—that meant they wouldn't be talking and his lover wouldn't be trying to kick him out.

He gave a little sob and wrapped himself around Morrie. He wanted to cry when Morrie's softened cock slipped free. Dutch rolled them over so Morrie could lay on him. He was just a bit bigger and didn't want to crush Morrie.

Neither of them said anything, Dutch was finally getting his breathing and emotions under control. He'd warned himself this wasn't just about sex and he hoped against all odds that this wasn't Morrie's way of saying goodbye forever. He wouldn't be able to handle a life with no Morrie in it. The last month had shown him that.

It wouldn't last, but he still wasn't ready for it to end.

"This was a bad idea." Morrie sighed.

"No, it was a great idea. I'm not going anywhere, Morrie. I love you."

"You can't stay here. We both know it. You've already been out of Zero Ward for too long."

"Let me worry about that."

"I can't. And you know they can't find you here. Not with what I'm carrying. It's too important." Morrie moved his hands to Dutch's chest and rested his chin there.

God, those dark brown eyes were so beautiful. Dutch could stare at them all day, but right now they looked sad and he hated that.

"I'm not going to jeopardize anything." Dutch soothed a hand down Morrie's back, caressing his soft skin. He missed these moments the most. Many an evening had been spent like this, laying and talking about things.

"You never mean to, but it happens. They like to fuck with you. Set an example." Morrie shrugged.

There was nothing he could do about that. When the family had found out about his proclivities, he was on the outs. He was always on the watch to see if someone would drag him out in public to show others what not to do. The gangs were all about keeping people in line.

"Doreen is on the gate."

"How much do you trust Doreen?"

"With my life, or I wouldn't be here."

"Is that who you trusted last time?"

"No, that ass got transferred. He thought he'd get promoted if he snitched, but that didn't happen. He got beaten almost as bad as I did." Dutch winced. He shouldn't have brought that up. Fuck. "Anyway, Doreen is family. She's got our back."

Morrie rolled off and got to his feet. Dutch sat up and clutched his legs, watching Morrie pace back and forth.

God, this part was hard. He ran a hand over his head and focused on the prickle. He needed to shave soon. He liked his head smooth. That took his attention for about a second before he looked back at Morrie. His lover was working up a good steam and he had to stop it before it got into the danger zone.

"I will go back to Zero Ward, but first I want to know that we're good. Don't leave me, Mor. I don't think I could handle that."

"It isn't like we're really together, Dutch. We have meetings."

"That's something, right? Maybe with this information you have, we can get more. I'd transfer over here in a heartbeat, but you know it will never be allowed, and there is no way I want you in Zero. It's one of the worst wards. Why do you think I was thrown there? If not for Doreen, I'd be dead and we wouldn't have met."

"Don't you see a theme here, Dutch? The family wants you dead and they will take any opportunity to do it, especially if it shows others how powerful they are."

Chapter Three

Moran couldn't understand why Dutch wouldn't listen to him. The whole situation was sucktastic. He could live with knowing Dutch was alive, even if they weren't together, but he couldn't live with the knowledge that he was part of the reason Dutch was dead. If they kept up this relationship, Dutch was going to be killed. He knew it in his heart. If they could wait—see if the information blew up the gangs—that would be something. Maybe they could be free, in the same ward. He had a sliver of hope.

"So we'll be more careful. I won't come to Ward Two anymore. We'll meet in Ward Zero, but close to the gates."

"How is that any better? You should give up your seat in the resistance and keep low. You're playing with fire."

"Will you come keep low with me?" Dutch's voice was low and uncertain.

Moran couldn't look at him. He kept moving. It had been a mistake to have sex. It had broken down some of the walls he was trying so hard to keep up.

He should have marched Dutch right back to Ward Zero.

"You know I can't. Not right now. Frankie needs me and who knows what that package will do once it's out in the open. Please. Go home. Forget about me. For now. Maybe—I don't know. This is so fucked up, Dutch."

Moran continued to pace back and forth across the living room. He should have been tired like he usually was after phenomenal sex, but he was too keyed up.

Dutch stood in his path as he turned for another journey across the room.

"Listen to me. Are you listening? I love you. I am not leaving you unless I'm dead. I know that scares you, but I am careful. Cesar wouldn't have me as part of the resistance if he didn't trust that I could do my job. So I'm a punching boy for the gangs, I can deal with that. They aren't going to kill me. Not now. Hurt me maybe, for fun, but I can handle that."

"But I can't, Dutch. Do you know how it broke me not being able to do a thing as they dragged you away from me? And not to hear from you for *two* weeks? I was a mess. Frankie had to drug my ass so I could sleep. If you're safe and I know you are, I can be good. Will I be happy? Fuck no. I want you with me here forever, but we can't have that so stop this. Now. We can't. Fuck. Dutch, I love you so much it hurts and I hate doing this. I hate knowing we can't be together and live a happy life. God. Dutch." Moran pulled at his hair. He hoped Dutch didn't touch him because he would fall even more apart. Everything about it was hard, but it had to be done.

Fuck. Shit. God damn it.

He had one happy place and it was Dutch, but now he had to give it up again and it was going to kill him.

"Stop. Mor, baby, you've got to stop this. We'll figure it out. I promise."

Moran collapsed into Dutch's arms and beat on his chest.

"You can't promise me that. If we're caught things could get worse and we don't know what kind of information we have. It might not help."

"Stop being so negative."

"One of us has to. You don't think of the consequences of your actions. This stolen moment right now? If you're found here you could die."

"I could die walking home from work."

"Don't joke about this shit." Moran pushed Dutch away and looked around for his pants.

After finding them he jerked them on, leaving them unbuttoned he looked for his shirt. His soul was already naked he didn't need his body to be as well.

"Who's joking? It's the truth. The enforcers get worse every day. The hard cases get pushed into Zero. We both know the gangs want that part of Chicago off the map. This 'reform' might make Zero obsolete, then were will I be? Relocate? Do you really think the gangs are going to spend their money getting people to move? No. It's more dangerous right now just to be in Zero Ward and I think the people know it. Just yesterday there was a riot in the street. Five people died and there was nothing I could fucking do. The only thing getting me through it? Thinking about you and being in your arms."

Moran turned to look at Dutch, his shirt still dangling from his fingers. He hated seeing him so defeated—his head was bowed and he rubbed at it, like he did when he was nervous.

"My love for you will always be there, Dutch. It isn't going anywhere. For now, we need to have space. If things open up—" He shrugged into his shirt and tried to button it only to remember it was ruined. He tugged it off then wadded it up, tossing it toward the kitchen.

Dutch strode over to him and shook him. "Don't you get it? If the reform goes through, there is a good chance I won't survive."

"What are you talking about? Maybe we can get you here in Ward Two and—"

"You forget, I was a part of the organization running Chicago. Not real high up, but high enough to know that relocate means they will probably gas all of Zero and we'll be relocated to a mass grave. Don't you understand? We need to take what time we have because we're fucking stuck here under the gangs' thumb."

"But the information. That has—"

"If it gets to where it needs to be in time. If they can fix it before the law goes in to effect. Will it be in time? I don't know. What I do know? I love you and I'm not losing the time I have. Don't you understand?"

"This whole thing is fucked. Damn it. We—"

Moran's phone rang, but it wasn't in his pocket. He looked around and spotted it on the floor. It could be Cesar or Frankie. Finally.

Dutch watched as Morrie answered the call. He hoped it was Cesar. The faster they got the ball rolling on this information, the better. It was getting too close to the bill being voted on and everyone knew it was just a formality. He should just go bomb the whole organization, but he'd never get close enough and too many innocent people could be hurt. At one point that wouldn't have phased him, but he'd changed so much in the time he'd been with Morrie. His moral compass was pointing the right way and he wouldn't move it back for anything.

He caught a few words here and there, but was trying to give Morrie his privacy. This was resistance business. He would be told what was going on. He put on his pants and looked at his shirt in disgust. He'd have to borrow something of Morrie's to get home and it was going to be tight. Good thing he had his trench coat.

" — okay. Yes. Bye."

"Frankie?" he asked. The conversation had been too informal to be Cesar. Usually Morrie would throw in a few 'yes sirs' if the head man was on the phone.

"Yes, I'm to head over tomorrow to hand off the information to a guy named Rory. We'll meet in Ward Three. One of the safe places there."

"Take me with you." God, if Morrie got hurt. Shit. Now Dutch knew how Morrie felt when thinking of him being hurt again. Everything about it was wrong. Stupid fucking gangs. If only they'd been born in another city — hell, state. There wasn't a lot of news from outside of Chicago, but enough leaked through to make him think other places were better. Of course — then there was the old grass is greener on the other side adage.

"Not going to happen. It's going to be hard enough for me to get over there with a day pass Cesar is going to get for me. This is going to move quick and I'd rather know you're at home in Ward Zero where they can't get to you."

"It's dangerous."

"Dutch, we're in the resistance against the most corrupt government in the country. Every breath we take is dangerous. And who are you to talk to me about danger? You are out of your ward. It was only last month you were dragged from here. Let's go. I'll walk you back. Make sure you get across okay." Morrie headed to the bedroom.

Probably to get a shirt. Dutch followed him because he needed to get dressed as well, he'd been gone too long as it was and he didn't want to get Doreen in trouble. The gangs could ping him at any time and if they found out she'd let him through, she wouldn't be transferred, she'd be dead.

"I don't want to leave like this." Dutch crowded Morrie against the dresser.

"You think I do? God, nothing is settled. I really don't want you going back to Zero right now. Not after you telling me how bad it is. If I could hide you here I would, but we're too close to making a change. We have to play this safe."

Dutch sighed in resignation. He hated everything about this. He should be the one in the danger zone, not Morrie.

"We aren't apart. I want you to know that. Our life might not be perfect right now, but we have our moments and I live for those. Don't take them away from me again." He wrapped his arms around Morrie.

Morrie turned and kissed him, lightly rubbing their lips together before just pressing them against each other. If he was going to cry it would have been now. This was bittersweet, almost like a goodbye.

Dutch closed his eyes and just let the moment wash over him, their lips not moving. He could feel a tear slip down Morrie's face. Fuck, this was hard. Maybe he shouldn't have come, but he did think Ward Zero was in a dead zone. If this was the last time they saw each other, it would be worth it for this second in time that he wished he could freeze. Dutch framed Morrie's face and wiped at the tears with his thumbs.

"I love you with everything that I am. Never forget that, Dutch," Morrie whispered against his mouth before he moved away.

Morrie rummaged through the dresser, pulled out a couple of shirts then tossed a black one at Dutch. It would be tight, but would work. He pulled it on and waited for Morrie to look at him.

"I love you too, and I want you to be extra careful tomorrow. Call me when you get back. Okay?"

"I will."

"And don't cut me out again."

"I won't."

"Good." He tugged Morrie close enough to press a hard kiss to his mouth before going to the living room. He needed his gun and to get his shoes back on. This was one of the hardest things he'd ever done. Leaving now wasn't a great idea, but they had no choice really. He wanted to stay the night and wake up with Morrie in his arms. Until the gangs were brought down, it just wasn't going to happen.

"You ready?" Morrie was adjusting his own gun.

"Just a sec." Dutch found his shoes and stomped into them.

Morrie handed over his shoulder strap and Dutch took it, strapping it on before getting his coat over it. It wasn't safe enough at night to travel without some kind of weapon. Enforcers looked the other way when people got mugged. If it didn't involve the gangs they stayed out of it—well, they'd take a cut from the thief, but that was about it. It was getting worse by the day. The police force was a joke and no one really called on them.

"We can take my car so we don't have to walk the whole way, but we'll have to ditch it a bit from the gate."

"Not the first time we've done this." Dutch winked at Moran.

"Right." Moran laughed.

He loved that sound and wanted to hear more of it.

"I'm ready."

Dutch followed Moran out of the door and hoped it wasn't the last time he'd be in the apartment.

Chapter Four

Moran led the way to his car. It was a piece of shit but got him around the ward when he needed it to. Most of the time he walked—it was good for him. Kept his mind from wandering. Driving gave him too much time to think and that past month he hadn't needed to be thinking about things.

He also didn't want to take Dutch back to Ward Zero, not after all the revelations he'd had today. He wouldn't put it past the gangs to eliminate people. They didn't care as long as they had what they wanted, and the resistance had been putting a lot of kinks in their plans, getting people riled up. So far his brother had stayed under the radar. Cesar was very good at keeping the top members of the resistance in the shadows so they could do their jobs.

He opened the door for Dutch then headed to the driver side. It was an hour or so to the closest gate. As long as that was the one Dutch had gone through. He hoped it was. No way had he taken a cab because it would have required ID and a check of his papers.

Moran usually didn't ask how Dutch got around the wards.

"Which gate did you come through?" Moran started the car, but didn't drive off yet.

"The one not far from here. Doreen had it today." Dutch buckled his belt and settled into his seat.

Moran could look at him all day, but they had things to do and sitting around in the car wasn't going to get them done. He'd rather be taking Dutch back upstairs and he would, if it hadn't gotten so late. The check point would close soon and Dutch couldn't be caught on this side.

"She'll still be on?" Moran shifted into drive.

Dutch looked at his watch and nodded.

That was good, one less thing for Moran to worry about. Moran put the car back in park and turned to Dutch. He had to say this one last thing. It was important to him that Dutch knew how much he was loved. If this was the last time they saw each other... He had to put it out there, because if it was, it meant one of them was dead. All the better to get his thoughts out there.

"I don't want to give up on us no matter how much I think this is dangerous. I wanted to wait until something was done with the gangs, but—life is too short. We both know that. I won't send someone else to our meetings, but you have to promise to keep a low profile and if you get wind of something happening you get to me. You got that? You get to me, no matter how hard it might be." Moran held out his hand.

Dutch took it and squeezed.

"You've got a deal. And you have to promise to take whatever precautions you can tomorrow."

That wouldn't be a hard promise to keep. He'd get his day pass and it would be smooth sailing. They were hard to come by, but Cesar could be trusted. He let go of Dutch's hand and checked his pocket. The information was still there. He didn't want to risk it being anywhere but on his person. The enforcers could randomly check people's apartments and that was a chance he wasn't going to take.

He drove toward the check point. The only noise was the music from the radio. For a few moments neither spoke—but he had more to say, so Moran turned down the radio, keeping it low for background noise.

"I let you go. I didn't want to, but I thought it was for the best. Thank you for not giving up." Moran took a quick glance at Dutch before turning back to the road.

"You never really let me go, sweetheart, because I was going to hang on until the end." Dutch kissed him on the cheek.

Moran laughed. "So you hold all the cards in this relationship, is what you're saying?"

"Not at all, but I figured I could show you the error of your ways. I mean—who could resist this?"

"You're so full of it." Moran snorted.

He hadn't felt this happy in over a month. Dutch always put him in a good mood and knew what to say to get him to relax. He could be a bit tense.

"You love everything about it."

"You know I do. It's been a long month." Moran sighed.

"That is has, but we have another meeting in a couple days," Dutch assured him.

"It's too long." He was starting to get sad again and he couldn't let it take over. This was supposed to be a happy moment. He wasn't giving Dutch up. They would make this work.

"I agree — I'd see you every day if I could. You know it."

"One day."

"Yes, one day. Soon."

They reached a good spot to stop the car. The rain had started on their drive. It was starting to come down harder, but they had no choice, they had to walk to the check point. The car would be tagged if it got too close and he would need that car for tomorrow. It was better to walk some of it with Dutch and let him go to the gate on his own. It wouldn't be the first time they'd done this, but it got harder every fucking time.

He got out of the car and they'd walked about a mile when his phone rang. He picked it up. It was Frankie again.

"Hey, what's up?"

There was static on the line and he was having a hard time hearing his brother.

"Trouble — Ward — get —" The phone went dead.

"That was odd. Frankie called. He was saying something about —"

He was thrown as if someone had pulled a string attached to his back.

Dutch froze. The rain poured around them, but he couldn't move. Moran had been on the phone just a second ago. Then... Dutch blinked, but it didn't go away. Everything was in slow motion. Moran had dropped his phone and jerked, falling to the ground.

He ran, but it felt like he was walking. Dutch rounded the car, a hot pain creasing his cheek. Dutch crouched behind the car and crawled to Moran.

"No, no, no." This couldn't be happening. Not now. If anyone was hurt it was supposed to be him. Not Morrie. "Fuck, fuck. Can you hear me?"

More shots were fired and he had no idea where they were coming from. What was going on? He'd heard nothing about enforcers being out today. The rain came down hard.

"Hurts." Morrie clutched at his chest and coughed.

No blood showed up in Morrie's mouth so he'd take that at as plus. For now.

"Oh, thank you baby Jesus. You're alive."

Footsteps echoed and Dutch had to make a decision. The gate was still too far away. There was no way he'd make it carrying Morrie. Not with someone out there shooting. He had to take care of the threat first. Which meant he had to leave Morrie, and he had no idea how bad he was hurt. He couldn't leave him exposed either. It was cold and raining.

A hard object was placed in his hand. Morrie's gun. He couldn't take it—that was the only thing standing between Morrie and whoever was out there gunning for them.

"Go kill those fuckers and get—fuck, shit—back here. God damn that hurts." Morrie coughed again.

They needed to get him out of the rain. Did he have time?

"I can't leave you out—"

"Fucking go before they get back here and kill us both."

Dutch searched the ground for Morrie's phone.

"You call your brother," he insisted. They might need help. He pressed the cell into Morrie's hand.

"Phone—connection—" The phone dropped back to the pavement.

Shit. Morrie had passed out. Dutch wanted to press against the wound to stop the blood, but there wasn't time. He took a deep breath and stood. Both guns in his hands, ready to take action. His trench coat flared behind him. It would have been very dramatic if the rain wasn't pounding away at him. A movement to his left had him swinging that direction. He aimed and shot. A thud sounded. He'd hit his mark. He'd take that bit of luck, because that wasn't skill. Not in this mess. He wiped his arm over his eyes, clearing his vision enough to look around—seeing if there was another shooter.

The crunch of footsteps had him moving to the other side of the car. No way was he letting anyone get to Morrie. He would protect him with his very life.

And there the shooter was. The idiot was in a white shirt that stood out like a beacon in the dark night. Dutch took aim and fired. A red spot blossomed on the shirt and the guy fell.

Dutch ran to the first guy. He was an enforcer in uniform. Something was wrong. He put a booted foot on the guy's chest in case he felt like moving. He had to know why they were this close to the gate and shooting.

"Why are you here?" He nudged with his foot, digging it into the would-be assassin's chest.

The guy shook his head and moved to grab Dutch's boot.

He dug it in harder. He needed answers damn it. Were they after Morrie or him? Fuck, if Morrie was shot because of him Dutch would never forgive himself. Damn it. After all the talk about love being the end all be all and that they would be together, this had to happen. Fuck.

"You'll answer or I'll kill you." He pointed his gun at the enforcer's head.

"I'm already dead. Do your worst." The guy sneered at him.

Dutch shrugged and pulled the trigger. He should have felt guilt as the hole appeared in the man's head, but he didn't. Enforcers wouldn't talk and he'd shot Morrie. The guy was right—he would have been dead anyway.

Now for the other idiot who couldn't be an enforcer unless he was out of uniform. Maybe Dutch would have better luck with him. When he got there the guy was attempting to crawl away. Dutch put a boot to his ass and shoved.

"Oh fuck, man, that hurts. Stop."

"You won't have to worry about hurting soon because you'll be dead unless you talk to me."

"Man, there was shooting, I just had my gun and—"

"Try again." Dutch pushed at the guy's ass again until he fell onto the ground.

"It's true. Shit. Get me to the hospital."

"Hurry up and tell me what I need to know or I'll shoot you in the head."

"What'll you do with the bodies? You can't bury us both."

"Let me worry about it. What do you know?"

"Nothing man. Seriously. I was told to be here and watch out for the guy in the black trench. That's all I know. I'm an informant, man. That's it. I didn't shoot nobody. I didn't."

"The gate is that way." Dutch pointed with is gun. "I suggest you start crawling."

"You can't leave me here. I'll die."

"I don't fucking care." Dutch turned his back and strode to the car.

Morrie hadn't moved from where he'd left him. He had to get him out of the rain. Fuck. He hadn't had time to really process what was happening, it had been over so quickly. But his lover was in the street fucking bleeding while he was off questioning people. He should have been taking care of Morrie.

He holstered his gun then reached for his cell phone so he could put a call in to Frankie. He knelt down and pulled Morrie onto his lap first.

"Dutch?"

"I'm here, baby. Don't talk. I got ya."

"Here. Safe."

It was the package. He put it into an inner pocket in his coat.

"We need to get you to a hospital."

"Can't."

"What the fuck to you mean, can't?"

"They'll know. Take me to Frankie."

"I don't care who fucking knows, you need medical attention."

Morrie clutched at Dutch's shirt. "You—get that where it need—fucking hell that hurts—Ward Three."

"Don't worry about that right now."

"Have to. For us. Call Frankie."

Dutch pressed against the wound hoping to stop the flow of blood. He used his other hand to dial his phone.

"Dutch, *what the fuck is happening?*" Frankie all but screamed into the phone.

"Frankie. It's Morrie. Fuck—he's been shot."

"Where."

"By the first gate to Zero."

The phone clicked.

Chapter Five

Moran hurt all over. He'd been shot. Fucking shot. They'd been right by the gate. A few more minutes and Dutch would have checked in through the other side. It was meters away and he had to fucking get shot. And he hadn't been alone. It took a minute for that to fully sink in.

"Dutch!" He shot upright in bed and clutched at his chest. It throbbed in pain.

He glanced down at himself to see he was in bed. How had he gotten there? The last thing he remembered was lying in the rain with his blood getting all over the place. He'd been so cold and worried. Dutch had been hovering over him and he'd been calling Frankie.

"He's fine."

Moran turned his head to see his brother sitting in a chair beside the bed—but no Dutch.

"Where am I?"

"Doesn't it look familiar? My place—and don't you ever fucking do that to me again. God damn it, Mor." Frankie reached out like he was going to slap him on the back of the head, but he pulled his hand back at the last minute.

"It wasn't my fault." Moran was whining, but he didn't care—he hurt, damn it. He lay back down and pressed a hand to his chest. It still hurt. Fuck, he needed drugs.

"I know." Frankie sighed. "But you've got to be more careful."

He peered over at his brother. His dark hair was all messed up like he'd run his hands through it a couple of hundred times and his eyes seemed tired. His face was drawn—a bit pale too. Something was wrong. If it wasn't Dutch, what could it be? It could be worry over him, but he couldn't be hurt that bad.

"Where's Dutch?"

"He's on his way to Third Ward."

"What!" Moran sat back up and grimaced. It hurt to move.

Shit, that was enough to worry anyone. Dutch wasn't a low man on the totem pole, he shouldn't be doing a drop this dangerous. Someone else should have been out there doing it. Fuck, it should have been him. Fuckers. It was supposed to be an easy drop for him, but now he was laid up in bed and Dutch was in danger.

"You heard me. It wasn't like you could take it, and Dutch wasn't going to let it go. I tried to tell him I have people who could handle it, but he feels responsible for this." Frankie waved a hand toward Moran. "Said for Cesar to get him the pass and he was going."

"Someone might recognize him. Hell—they were waiting for us at that fucking gate."

"You think we don't all know that. In fact, that's almost exactly what I said to your damn boyfriend, but the asshole never listens to anybody."

"So what happened?" He eased back down onto the bed. He really didn't want to move again anytime soon.

"Someone spotted Dutch here in our sector. An enforcer was sent to the gate to wait for him." Frankie shrugged.

Like it was no big deal, but it was. No one should have been on to Dutch. Moran knew someone had it out for his lover, but this fucking sucked.

"Doreen?"

He hoped it wasn't the person Dutch had said was family. That would break his lover's heart like nothing else would. It was different if it just was a no name snitch giving someone over to the enemy.

"It wasn't her. She's fine. It was someone over here, I think. I'm not hundred percent sure. We took care of the body and got you here. The doc worked you over and said you'd live. You'll be a little sore, but the bullet was a through and through and it missed anything important. You were lucky it was raining. Enforcers usually don't miss."

"Well—I hate to say this, but I look nothing like Dutch. Not even in the dark. Why'd they shoot me?"

"I can't answer that. Dutch couldn't get anything out of either guy. We've got the survivor in custody for now. He isn't saying a word. He's innocent in all of this." Frankie snorted. "Innocent men aren't out on the street pointing guns at people."

"Is he an enforcer?"

"Dutch said he was a snitch. He could have been the one who spotted Dutch coming out of Zero Ward. I don't think we'll ever really know." Frankie shrugged.

"He can't go back there."

He didn't need to tell his brother he was talking about Zero Ward. There was no way Dutch would be safe in that area anymore.

"They'll be looking for him soon. You're right, if he goes back they'll kill him. Especially when the enforcer doesn't show. He's been out of the sector for too long."

"Fuck. What're we going to do?" Moran closed his eyes and leaned his head back.

It was too much. They'd gone from not seeing each other, to the hope of weekly meetings, to Dutch being on the run. It'd been a hell of a day. Well—now he was on day two of the fucktastic adventure he never wanted to be on.

"I already talked to Cesar. Once Dutch gets the information passed along we're smuggling you two out of Chicago."

"How? That almost never works. What will we do when we leave?"

"Cesar knows some people on the outside. They'll set you up. If we can get the gangs out of power you guys can come back, but until then I don't want to see your face again."

"Frankie—"

"It's for the best. I should have gotten you out of here after the folks died, but I needed you too much. I'm sorry." Frankie laid his hand on Moran's shoulder.

"Don't. You did the right thing. I don't want to leave now." Moran reached up and squeezed Frankie's hand.

"You don't have a choice. Not if you want any kind of life with Dutch." Frankie squeezed back then moved away.

"Frankie, I need you too," Moran whispered.

"I know you do, kiddo, but right now you and Dutch need each other more. I can't go through this again. I knew it was a possibility when I made you my right hand man, but this is too much. So it's final. Tomorrow you'll be on your way to a new life out of this shit."

* * * *

Dutch waited behind a tree. He was scoping out the gate that would get him to Third Ward. He knew it was risky, but this was his mission now. Moran had been hurt because of him and he was going to get the job done. He'd waited until the doctor had said Morrie would be okay before issuing his orders. He should have asked, but in the state he was in he couldn't be nice about it. Cesar didn't like it, but he was letting Dutch have this one. Come hell or high water, Cesar knew Dutch would complete his task.

The worker he was eyeing yawned. He was pretty sure it was the guy he was supposed to go through. He looked bored and from the intel, all Dutch had to do was slip him a bit of money if the guy got suspicious and he'd be through. If anyone spotted him on the street he had his day pass in his pocket. He hoped not to be stopped but he had to account for everything. It wasn't like he was a big family member who could go wherever he wanted to. They had flexible rules. The power had totally corrupted this bunch. His own great-great grandfather had been one of those members. It was the only reason he'd been punished by being exiled to Zero Ward instead of being killed outright. They were hoping he'd end up dead, but not by their hand. They had some honor, if misconstrued. And he'd had Doreen. His great aunt. If not for her, he would have died that night. He was so thankful she hadn't been hurt last night when the guns had started to fire. He'd checked on her while the medics were looking over Moran.

He counted himself lucky, but was beginning to think it had run out. He strolled up to the gate and showed his pass. The guard looked him up and down, but before he could say anything Dutch slipped him a fifty.

The guard waved him through. It seemed too easy. He hoped Moran was doing well. Dutch knew Frankie would take care of Moran, but he sort of wished he would be there when his lover woke up, not Frankie. To tell him the good news.

Now if only he made it through this task alive. He was regretting not taking Frankie up on his offer to have one of his other people handle the drop, but he knew how important this was to Moran. He'd want to know it was done and if Dutch had stayed at Frankie's house he would have had them out of the city right then and there.

Each Ward had a different feel, but for the most part they looked the same. Some were more rundown than others, like his ward. He'd have to let his second in command know what was going on, but he could do that when he got back to Frankie's place.

The safe place was another drugstore. He had no idea why the resistance chose them other than it had supplies they needed. Most of the workers were resistance, but not all of the customers, so they still had to be careful. If they didn't have a reason to be there they'd be interrogated and that was never pretty. He'd been a part of a few of those in his time.

He was happy it wasn't a part of his life anymore. He'd kill when he had to, but it was a matter of life and death these days, not an order from above.

He walked a few miles. The place was a good hour inside the gate. He was tired, but wouldn't let it slow him down. He had a lover to see when this was finished. Lost in thought, he almost didn't see the enforcer coming his way. A quick turn to the left put him out of sight. It was close, but the guy must not have seen him. He kept walking only to bump into another enforcer coming the other way.

Why was this zone so full of enforcers today? He kept his head down and tugged on his hat.

"Excuse me. Sorry about that. Day pass, you know? Seeing the sites—good behavior and all." He rambled along and kept walking.

"Just watch where you're going." The enforcer cuffed him in the head.

Dutch wanted to punch back, but instead nodded and kept walking. This wasn't about him. It was about the needs of the people and he wasn't going to fuck that up. Not so close to having something he'd never dreamed he'd have. A full life with Moran Schultz. That was worth fighting for, even if it took him to a place that was so far out of his comfort zone. He was nervous, but would do anything to be with Moran.

After the run in with the enforcer he was more alert. He couldn't afford a fuck up this close to the finish line. Cesar had given him a brief description so he knew who to look for. He walked into the drugstore and headed to the back. The guy was supposed to be in the magazine section, and sure enough there he was.

Dutch moved beside him and picked up a magazine. He had the package in his hand.

"This is a good one." He passed it along.

The contact didn't say anything, just nodded and accepted the information. And just like that, it was over. His part in this was complete. He nodded back and turned away. He picked up a water bottle—it had been a long walk—and moved to the register to pay.

He hoped, when all was said and done, that everything they'd gone through would be worth it. That the little people would win and the families would be on their asses and brought down with the justice they deserved.

For now, he had a man to see about a new life.

Chapter Six

Moran was beyond anxious. It was getting late and Dutch wasn't back yet. Tired and cranky, all he wanted to do was sleep, but he couldn't get comfortable — not knowing what was going on wasn't helping. How long did it take to make the freakin' drop? Not like he had a clock or anything in the damn room. It was like the forces were conspiring against him. All he wanted to do was see Dutch with his own eyes to make sure he was okay.

The door creaked open and he looked over, hoping it was Dutch, but it wasn't. His brother had a tray with some food on it. Not that he was hungry. He was too nervous to eat. Well — until he got a whiff of whatever his brother had brought in. His stomach actually growled.

"Nice to see you're hungry."

"Any news?"

Frankie shook his head. "Not yet. It's still early. He'll be back."

"You're not just saying that to placate me are you?" Moran arched an eyebrow.

"No. If something had gone down, you'd be the first I told."

Moran knew that, but he just wanted this day over. For Dutch to be right there with him, in the bed talking about what happened next.

"You need to eat and try to get some rest. I'll send Dutch in as soon as he gets back. Tomorrow is going to be a long day and with your injury, it is going to be hard as well." Frankie set the tray down on the bedside table and kissed Moran's forehead.

It was a gesture he used to do all the time when Moran had been a kid. He was going to miss his brother something fierce. They could still call each other. The gangs weren't that great at monitoring frequencies, and the resistance had been one step ahead of them in that department. So it wasn't like he would never talk to his brother again, but it might be a really long time until they saw each other.

"I love you."

"Love you too, bro. Now get to eating. I have a few more things to get in order before we move you."

Frankie shut the door behind him. Moran might as well eat—it would keep his mind off Dutch for a bit. Not for long, though, because now that they had a chance at a new life it was all he could think about. He would have never thought he'd be happy to leave Chicago. It was his home. Second Ward was all he'd ever known. The mobsters had been in control for so long people had forgotten how it was to live in a place with justice. He wondered what it would be like on the outside. Moran figured each place had its own downfalls.

He was finishing his sandwich when the door opened again. This time it was Dutch. He let out a breath. He'd been so tense and now it drained from his body.

"You made it."

"You're awake."

They spoke at the same time. Moran laughed. God it was good to see that face.

"The drop went okay?" Moran asked as Dutch sat down in the chair by the bed.

"It was as smooth as could be. The information is now in the hands of Third Ward."

"Good. One step closer to being free."

"Yes it is. More so for us. Are you ready for this? I assume your brother told you the plan?" Dutch was on the edge of the seat.

Moran pushed the tray to the table and scooted over before patting the bed.

"Come here."

"I don't want to hurt you."

"Everything hurts right now. You sitting on the bed won't even rate. Come here."

Dutch slowly sank down beside him. Moran laid his head on his lover's shoulder. He winched a bit as they both shifted to get comfortable.

"I shouldn't be—"

"Yes, you should. I'm fine and I need you here where I can touch you."

Moran closed his eyes and just focused on both of their breathing. Dutch was his and they wouldn't be parted again if he had anything to say about it.

"So, what do you think? No more Chicago."

"I'll miss Frankie, but I'm ready to be out of here so we can be together. You know—love don't die, baby, and you are stuck with me from here on out."

Dutch snorted and it jostled Moran a bit. He clinched his teeth, but didn't make a sound because there was no way he wanted Dutch to get up from the bed.

He didn't have to worry, Dutch nuzzled into his throat, leaving wet kisses along the length.

"Watching you fall last night—that about ended me. Right then and there."

"It came out of nowhere. I was standing there one minute and the next I was on the ground bleeding."

"Only one of us is allowed to get hurt in this relationship and it isn't you. Never again."

"Ha! Neither of us is going to get hurt again."

"You can't say that, Morrie. We don't know what we are going into on the outer walls. Who knows, it could be worse than the situation we're in now."

"No. It won't be. Frankie was telling me a bit about Indiana. That's where we're headed. Close enough, yet far enough away. That's our first stop anyway. They don't have mobsters or gangs running the show there."

"What about the whole gay thing?"

"That I'm not too sure about, but we're not being parted again. If we have to, we move on until we find a place we can be happy."

"And what about Chicago?"

"What about it? The only thing holding me here is Frankie. Hell, if I could, I'd get him to go with us."

"I know you would, baby." Dutch kissed his cheek.

"You missed." Moran turned and kissed Dutch, running his tongue over the seam of his lips.

"You're hurt," Dutch mumbled into the kiss.

Moran took advantage of the situation and swept his tongue inside, taking the kiss deeper. The way he was sitting started to hurt. He had to move. He released Dutch and panted, clutching at his chest.

"I knew this was a bad idea."

"No, it wasn't. We both need this. I just can't turn like that. It hurts too much."

"Okay. I have an idea. Let me lock the door." Dutch got off the bed to do his bidding.

Before he came back he took off his clothes and set them on the chair. Moran just had his underwear on and he stretched to take them off, but it hurt. He lay back down.

"You don't even twitch. I've got this."

Moran nodded and adjusted himself so he was flat on the bed. He closed his eyes and let Dutch take care of him. The blanket was taken off him and there was a slight chill in the room. He didn't care because soon his underwear was tossed aside. He heard them hit the floor.

"Now, don't tense up."

Moran nodded and did his best to relax. He took a deep breath then released it when Dutch wrapped his lips around Moran's cock. He tensed.

"Fuck."

"I said don't move or I'm stopping."

"Don't stop." His dick had softened a bit after he'd shifted, but it didn't take long for Dutch to get it back to hard and ready to go.

"Nice and easy," Dutch whispered.

Moran moaned his response. Warm heat surrounded him. He wanted to look down to watch, but that would put him in a position that might hurt and there was no way he wanted this to stop. Dutch cupped his balls and gave him a light squeeze. He was so close. He shouldn't be, but just knowing Dutch was there taking care of him had him on the edge.

"Close, baby." Moran licked his lips and wished Dutch was closer so he could kiss him.

Dutch scraped his teeth lightly along his shaft and sucked him down before swallowing around Moran's erection. He was done. He came and clinched his abdomen, putting a bit of pressure on his chest. It hurt, but not enough for him to make this stop.

"Dutch, I love you. Mmmm. Yes."

His lover continued to suck on the tip of his cock until he was spent. Dutch got off the bed and maneuvered so he was once again beside Moran.

"What about you?"

"I came when you did."

"What?"

"Don't wiggle around. I just got you all relaxed. Seeing you alive and whole and tasting you was all I needed."

Moran rested his head on Dutch's chest feeling safe and secure. Maybe he was a bit anxious about the future, but that was a fate many others fared as well. They would be out from under the thumbs of the men who hated Dutch so much they wanted him dead.

Tomorrow was going to be a better day and he would face it with the love of his life. Hand in hand they would tackle whatever life threw at them and hopefully in the near future there would be a visit to Chicago to see Frankie. He didn't know if they would ever go back, but that was another problem for tomorrow.

PASSION UNDER FIRE

Stephani Hecht

Dedication

To Jackie, Jennifer and Theresa, the best
partners/friends ever.

Chapter One

Smack! The sound of flesh hitting flesh reverberated through the large office. Georgio barely held back a wince as he watched one of his good friends and closest allies, Dirk, take another blow from one of his brothers' enforcers. They had him on his knees right in front of Georgio's brothers' desks. They were both watching the show with cold smiles on their faces, their dark eyes intense as if they didn't want to miss a moment of the action.

As it was, Dirk was already bleeding from his now crooked nose, he had a split lip and his eyes were beginning to swell. It wouldn't take long before they expanded so much that Dirk wouldn't be able to see at all.

Thud! This time the blow hit Dirk on the jaw and sent him reeling to the side. Were it not for the two men holding him up, Dirk would surely have fallen to the floor. Georgio gritted his teeth together as rage boiled through him. At the same time, he held tight onto the arms of his chair. If his brothers really knew how close he and Dirk were, then things could get even worse.

The funny thing was, while Dirk and Georgio were both gay, they were far from being a couple. Sure, they had fooled around a few times. Every encounter had been awkward and unfulfilling for the both of them. So in the end they had decided that they made much better friends than lovers. Still, if Georgio's brothers were to catch wind of just how tight he and Dirk were, Georgio knew it would send them into a rage. They already suspected that Georgio was gay — this would be the fuel they needed to add to their great big gay fire. They were just looking for a way to confirm that Georgio was indeed gay. Then they would have a legitimate reason to off Georgio without pissing off the rest of the family members.

Whack! Yet another blow, this one hitting the side of Dirk's jaw. His blue eyes rolled into the back of his head, but he somehow managed to stay conscious. More blood began to run, mixing in with his blond hair.

What was Dirk's sin? The fucking irony of it all was that Dirk hadn't done a damn thing. It had been Dirk's youngest sister who had committed the transgression, and boy, was it a doozy. She had done something so dangerous that it had earned her a kill-on-sight order. She had joined the rebellion group that was determined to overthrow the gangs that ruled Chicago. But she was buried so far underground that the leaders of their gang, Georgio's older twin brothers, couldn't find her. They had decided to take out their frustration on the poor enforcer.

Georgio had to give big kudos to his friend — Dirk was taking the beating like a man. While he let out an occasional grunt, he never cried out. He never begged for mercy either. But that was Dirk, he was as stubborn as a mule and he would never give Michael or Luciano that satisfaction. He hated Georgio's brothers just as much as Georgio did. The only reason he worked for the twins was because it had kept his family safe…until now. That had all changed. Dirk would still be forced to work for the twins because Georgio knew that they would want to keep close tabs on him. Meanwhile, the rest of his family would be in trouble as well. Any one of them could *disappear,* and there was nothing that Georgio or Dirk could do about it. Damn it, life really sucked sometimes. The ironic thing was that Georgio didn't blame Dirk's sister. He just wished that he had the courage to do the same thing. He would love nothing more than to bring down his brothers and put an end to their tyranny.

When the enforcers finally let Dirk slide to the ground, Georgio released a sigh of relief. That meant that they were going to let his friend live. Yeah, they might have beaten the hell out of him, but he would eventually heal and be his old self. Dirk wasn't going to let something like a beating break him. He was too strong for that.

"Are we done here?" Georgio drawled, trying to make it sound as if he didn't give a damn about what had just happened.

"Why? You have someplace to go?" Michael snapped.

Like all the brothers in the family, Michael had short black hair and brown eyes. While the twins preferred to slick theirs back with enough gel to supply their entire district, Georgio preferred to keep his free. Sure, it meant that the front of it tended to flop in his face, but Georgio would do anything to distance himself from his brothers. Even if it was a silent protest of not styling his hair like theirs.

Georgio despised his brothers, almost as much as he hated the whole gang life. All it led to was blood, meaningless loss of lives, and unnecessary heartbreak. Georgio was sick of seeing people like his brothers continue to get richer, whereas most of the rest of the district continued to grow poorer. Every time Georgio drove through the city, he saw more homeless people. Many of them emaciated and dying. How was that fair?

The door opened, and a man walked inside. Georgio sucked in a breath. He'd never seen a more gorgeous looking person in his life. The newcomer looked to be about five years younger than Georgio, which would put him at around twenty. He wasn't dressed in fancy clothing—in fact, what he wore was next to rags. His pants were torn and had grease stains in many places. His shirt was in no better condition. It might have been white at one point, but it had been washed so many times it now was a faded gray. All of it screamed that this guy was a new recruit. Which made Georgio sad. Somebody so young shouldn't have to throw his life away to a gang just so he could survive.

The newcomer had short brown hair that was uneven in places. It announced *my mommy gave me this cut!* It still didn't take away from his good looks. Then he turned to look at Georgio, and that's when he saw the kid's best feature of all—his eyes. They weren't just blue, they were so intense that, when he shifted some in the lighting, they almost appeared violet.

Luciano let out a sigh. "What do you need now, Tito?"

Ahhh...so his name was Tito. Georgio let it roll around in his head. He wondered what it would feel like if he said it right before he kissed the man, held him, hell, did all kinds of things to him. It made Georgio hard just thinking about it, and he had to shift in his chair to hide his erection from the others.

Tito shot a nervous glance at Dirk before he held out a small envelope. Even from across the room, Georgio could tell that Tito's hand was shaking. It also told Georgio what Tito's new job was. He was the family's newest runner. His brother employed a number of them. Most of them were poor young men who had agreed to the jobs in the hopes of moving up in the ranks and getting better positions. Ones that paid a whole lot more money. Then they would be able to take care of themselves, instead of ending up on the streets, wasting away, like so many others.

Georgio felt a burst of frustration. It shouldn't be like this. Life should give the good a fair chance, not only the bad. Being a runner was a dangerous job. Often, wannabe opposing gangs would kill a runner and send the body parts back to the twins as a warning. Not that the twins ever took it seriously. They were too strong, too established for any gang to ever take them down. But that didn't keep the other gangs from trying.

Michael held out another envelope to Tito. This one was long and thin. "Take this to the bakery on the corner of First and Tenth. It's a little reminder that they're behind on their payment this month. Make sure they know that the next time we have to visit, it will be one of us and an enforcer who delivers the message."

Georgio's heart skipped a beat when he heard the location. The guy in question might seem innocent enough because he was just a baker, but he had sent more than one of the runners back bloodied and bruised. Georgio sure as hell didn't want to see the same happen to Tito. But how in the hell was he going to protect the younger man?

"I'll go with him," Georgio stated.

His brothers looked over at him in shock. Up until that moment, they had done their best to ignore him. Which was what they usually did. Not that Georgio minded. It made life much easier that way.

"Why is that?" Luciano asked, his eyes narrowing with suspicion.

"Because we all know if we send this runner, the baker won't take it seriously. He'll just beat Tito and send him back to us," Georgio replied with a heavy sigh.

"How is it that you know his name?" Michael demanded, looking just as suspicious as his twin.

Sometimes, Georgio wondered how it was that both of them had ended up so stupid. Seriously, it was a fifty-fifty shot that at least one of them would have some brains. Yet it took both of them to do the math to figure out how much they should leave as a tip for their server when they went out to eat.

The only reason they were the leading family in the district was because their father had fought his way to the top. Michael and Luciano sure as hell wouldn't have had the skill and brains for it. The only reason they were still on top was the fact that his brothers ruled with an iron fist. Georgio wondered just how long that tactic would work before another gang managed to knock them down a peg. He was willing to bet that it wouldn't be too long.

"I know his name because you mentioned it," Georgio reminded them as he fought hard not to roll his eyes. They always got pissed with him whenever he did that.

Michael stroked his chin thoughtfully. "You may have a point. If we send you, that may put some fear in the baker. It's getting to the point where I may just have to bring him in and off him myself."

A small gasp from Tito showed just how new to this world he was. Nobody else in the room was shocked or surprised with Michael's statement. They didn't keep a big roll of plastic in the closet for nothing. They usually carried out the executions in the office since Michael and Luciano got off on seeing the deaths themselves. Sick bastards that they were. As for Georgio, he usually did his best to avoid the office at those times. Some liked to call him weak, or a coward, or even a pansy for doing so. Georgio didn't give a damn. If he didn't have to see another death, he would take all the name-calling and then some.

Getting up, Georgio gestured for Tito to follow him. "Come on. Let's get this over with."

Chapter Two

As they walked down the street to the bakery, Tito couldn't help but shoot glances at Georgio. Tito knew he should be keeping his gaze down on the ground in a sign of subordination, but he couldn't help himself. Georgio was just too damn good-looking.

When Tito had been hired for the job, he'd been creeped out by the twins. With their slicked-back hair, narrowed brown eyes and dangerous vibe, Tito had almost run in the opposite direction. Then he'd remembered his little brother, Tommy, who was back home. That is, if they could call the shack they lived in a home. Not only was Tommy sick all the time, but Tito could see his brother wasting away. He wouldn't make it much longer unless Tito did something desperate.

As such, he had agreed to work for the twins as one of their runners. Yes, he knew what he was doing was illegal. He also knew it was dangerous. And that the pay wasn't the best. But at least it was better than nothing, and Tito could work his way up in the organization. Even if he hated the mobs.

It had been the gangs that had killed his mother and father, leaving Tito and Tommy to fend for themselves. It hadn't been easy. For a while, Tito had managed to keep them afloat with the small pittance they'd been given when their parents had died, plus the little Tito made working odd jobs here and there. But now, their little nest egg had dried up, and Tito was getting desperate. He also knew that he needed to get Tommy to a doctor sooner rather than later. Disease was running rampant in the ghetto were they lived. If Tito lost Tommy… Tito didn't think he could go through that kind of pain again.

Tito darted another quick glance at Georgio. He let his hair go free. Although it was still short, there wasn't a spot of gel in it. It fell in soft waves, the front flopping into his face a bit. It still didn't obstruct his dark brown eyes. While they were same color as his brothers', they didn't have the same predatory glare in them. There was a hint of kindness. Something that Tito would have never imagined from one of the family members of the leading gang. Strange as it might seem, Tito almost felt safe in Georgio's presence.

"Do you want me to give you the envelope, sir?" Tito asked.

Gee, since when had his voice grown so high-pitched? Tito wanted to kick himself in own ass for sounding like such a dork. Georgio probably thought that Tito was some big doofus or something.

Who was he kidding? Georgio probably didn't even notice Tito at all. It was that way with all the gangsters. They looked at runners as human e-mails and nothing more. Heck, if the gangsters weren't so paranoid about having their computers hacked, they would probably do away with runners altogether. But then again, they would still need somebody to go around and collect the *protection* cash from the local merchants, so maybe they did need runners after all.

"You can go ahead and keep the envelope for now," Georgio said, his voice smooth like whiskey.

Not that Tito ever had the chance to drink whiskey on a regular basis. The only time he'd been able to taste it had been when the twins had given him a glass after they had hired him. It'd been their way of welcoming Tito into the gang. After that, they had pretty much ignored him with the exception of barking orders at him.

Tito always jumped to obey, too. During his first week there, he'd seen firsthand what happened when employees didn't obey the twins. Tito had gone in to deliver his day's drop. When he'd walked in, he'd seen one of the other runners kneeling on the ground. There'd been a piece of plastic under him. Tito had wondered why. Then the awful truth had come to him when Michael had pulled out a gun and shot the other runner in the head.

Tito had been so shocked, he'd jumped five feet. Then the smells of blood, charred flesh and gun smoke had hit him, and Tito had had to swallow several times to stop himself from vomiting right there on the carpet. Tito had done his very best to hold it in. Somehow, he had the feeling that staining the twins' carpet might get him his own piece of plastic.

Michael had turned to Tito. "Now you know what happens to those who try to skim off the top. Don't think you can fool us either — we'll find out one way or another."

As if! Tito now knew that the twins couldn't count higher than ten — twenty if they took off their socks. But they did have an accountant on staff, and he was great at his job and damn good at finding out any suspicious activity.

Tito shivered as he brought his thoughts back to the present. There was no reason to believe that the same fate awaited Tito. Not if he kept his head low, was respectful and didn't try any funny stuff. He couldn't die. If he did, then there would be nobody left to take care of Tommy.

"So what made you decide to get into this work?" Georgio asked.

The question startled Tito. Nobody in the gang had ever really given a shit as to why he wanted the job. Not even the twins had asked when they hired him. They had been too busy leering at Tito to even think of that.

Tito gave what he hoped was an indifferent shrug. "I just needed the money, like everybody else. I knew this would be the quickest way to do it."

The last thing Tito was going to reveal was that he had a sick brother at home he desperately needed to take care of. That would only give the gang one more thing to use against him should they ever get angry at him. Tito never wanted to put Tommy in any kind of danger. It had been Tito's decision to take this job, not Tommy's. In fact, Tommy hated that Tito was working for the gang. When he had found out, he'd had a total fit. While Tommy might be sick and needing care, he was eighteen years old and he knew how things in the streets worked.

Georgio didn't seem to buy Tito's explanation, though. Georgio gave Tito a suspicious look as he slowly shook his head. "Why do I have a feeling there's more to the story than just that?"

A fluttering sensation built up in Tito's stomach. "I don't know because that's all there is to it. My life, plain and simple. I'm just another one of the bottom of the barrel guys, just struggling to survive."

"Okay, we'll leave it for now," Georgio said, but there was something in the tone of his voice that told Tito that the gangster would be bringing up the topic again.

Tito let out a little sigh of relief. He was off the hook, for now at least. Eventually, Georgio would forget about Tito, since he was just one of many runners. Then Georgio would never bring up the question again.

As they reached the bakery, Tito's chest clenched in fear. The other runners had told him about the man that ran this place. He was mean as hell and sadistic as the devil himself. He'd smacked around more than one runner and usually spit on all of them when they came to pick up the weekly money. Tito was not looking forward to meeting him.

Sure enough, as soon as Tito walked into the bakery, a tall, bulky man with gray eyes turned on him. Even though the baker was behind the counter, Tito still felt like prey to a huge predator. So much so, that Tito walked back a couple of steps.

"Get the hell out of my shop. Tell those brothers that I'll pay when I'm damn well and ready!" the baker shouted.

Just as it looked as if he was about to spit on Tito, Georgio entered the bakery. The store owner's eyes grew large as his face paled so much it almost matched his hair. Tito had to bite on his bottom lip so he didn't do something stupid like laugh in the man's face.

"Georgio! I wasn't expecting to see you here today. What an honor," the baker gushed.

"I'm sure you weren't. Otherwise, you wouldn't be getting ready to spit on one of our runners or smack him around," Georgio replied in cool voice, as he put his hands in his black, tailor-made suit jacket.

"I was never going to do that."

"Sure, Maggio, why would I ever think that, since you've done it to every other runner we've sent to you before? In fact, it's happened so much that my brothers and I are beginning to see it as a personal insult to us. Now, you wouldn't want to be sending that kind of message would you? Michael and Luciano are about to come here themselves, and we all know that they don't play nearly as nice as I do."

Maggio looked so terrified that if he had pissed himself, Tito wouldn't have been surprised. As it was, the baker's face had turned from pale to green. Not that Tito blamed the poor bastard. He'd probably react the same way if he knew that he'd be expecting a visit from the twins.

Maggio reached under the counter and pulled out a fat envelope. With shaking hands, he gave it to Georgio. It was only then that Tito remembered that he had an envelope of his own to deliver.

"Excuse me, sir, but I was instructed to give this to you," Tito said.

Maggio took it from Tito, then opened it. It looked to be a photograph of some kind. When Maggio looked at it, his face became even greener and he let out a sob. Dropping the photograph, he began to shake his head several times as tears formed in his eyes.

Since the picture had floated to Tito's side of the counter, he bent down to pick up. It was a normal family picture. He recognized Maggio in it. A woman, most likely his wife, sat next to him, and they were surrounded by several children. A shiver went down

Tito's spine when he realized all of Maggio's family members had giant black Xs drawn over their eyes.

Georgio took the picture from Tito. He looked at it, then let out a low hiss of disgust. Balling up the offending photo, Georgio threw it into the nearest garbage bin.

"You need to stop play games, Maggio," Georgio said. "I know this is the busiest bakery in the district, so you should have no trouble paying on time. Why do you continue to give my brothers such a hard time?"

Maggio was silent for so long that Tito didn't think he was going to answer. Finally, the baker lifted his head. There was such raw hatred and anger in the man's eyes that it made Tito's stomach flip. "It's the only way I can get back at them."

"It's going to get you killed," Georgio said in a soothing voice. "I don't want that to happen to you. You have your family to think of. What would they do without you? I know the situation isn't fair and it sucks, but for right now, it's what we have to deal with."

"What do you mean *for right now*? It's always been this way, and it's never going to change," Maggio said, his voice cracking just a bit. "They'll always keep taking, and we'll always be stuck where we are."

Tito's heart broke for the man. At the same time, he got a sick sensation in his stomach. Did that mean that there was no way that he and Tommy would ever get out of the slums? Were they forever doomed to live in squalor? Would Tito have to watch as Tommy died a premature death, just because his brother couldn't get the most basic of medical care?

It was all so unfair. Tito wanted to lash out. He wanted to hit somebody. Preferably one of those rich, smug bastards. He wanted to beat them until they felt a little bit of the hate that Tito was experiencing at that moment. Sure, it would probably mean signing his own death warrant, but it would almost be worth it.

Georgio leaned over the counter and put a compassionate hand on Maggio's shoulder. "I know how much it sucks. If there was anything I could do to change it, I would."

"You can start by going to the bar between Second and Third this Tuesday at eight in the evening," Maggio said.

Georgio's eyes narrowed. "Why?"

"I know that you're nothing like your brothers. You hate being in their lifestyle. Plus I trust you, believe it or not. But I'm taking a big risk here. There are many lives at stake if you were to leak this information." Maggio shot a look at Tito. "Do you understand me?"

Tito nodded. "I never heard a word that was spoken in here. I'm just a runner that likes to keep his life simple."

Georgio studied Tito for several moments. "Maybe there is hope for you yet." He then turned to Maggio. "I'll be there, and I'll make sure I don't have a tail on me."

Georgio then grabbed Tito and practically dragged him out of the bakery. It was all Tito could do to keep from tripping as they left. Once they were out of the building, Georgio took Tito by the chin and forced him to lock gazes.

"You can't mention a word about this to Michael or Luciano. Not only could it get Maggio killed, but it could earn me a bullet in the head. Do you hear me?"

As if Tito wanted to be in the middle of that kind of mess. The further away from it, the better. "I won't say anything, I promise."

Georgio let Tito go. "I may be going crazy, but something tells me to trust you."

While Tito rubbed at his chin, Georgio reached inside his inner jacket pocket and pulled out a wad of bills. He then grabbed Tito's hand and pressed the roll into his palm. Tito looked down at the money in shock. There had to be over two hundred dollars there.

"Is this hush money?" Tito asked, slightly offended.

"No, it's for you to buy some decent clothing and get some food. I can't have one of my runners looking like he just crawled out of the slums."

With those parting words, Georgio turned around and walked away. Tito watched in stunned silence until the crowd swallowed Georgio and Tito couldn't see him anymore.

Chapter Three

Tito walked in a daze back to the home that he shared with Tommy. Like every other building on skid row, their place was made from the cheapest material possible. That meant the walls were thin, so they froze in the winter and baked in the summer. The roofs weren't any better. Every time it rained, they were forced to rush around with buckets and bowls to catch water from the various leaks. The floor was covered by thin carpet that didn't hold up to common use. It already had various holes in it, just from Tito and Tommy walking on it. Tito would hate to see how it would look if he were a tap dancer. They would be down to the concrete slab then.

He went up the wobbly front stairs, once again wincing at the color of the home. It was the same as all the others, but that still didn't stop Tito from hating it. It was a dull brown. It made the entire neighborhood look bleak and like it was dying. Which was really true, since there wasn't a day when one of the residents didn't die there.

Tito took in a deep breath. Well, that wasn't going to be his or Tommy's fate. Tito was determined that they were going to get out of this place. Even if it meant that they had to work for the very same people that put them there in the first place.

Sure, he hated it. It made him feel like a traitor. It even made him feel a little cowardly. Tito didn't care. There was no way he was going to stand by and watch Tommy die, be it because he was sick or from starvation. As the oldest, it was Tito's responsibility to take care of Tommy, and Tito was determined to do a good job of it.

As soon as Tito walked in, the smell of beans and rice hit him. Well, at least their meals were consistent. Tito didn't complain, though, because he knew that they were luckier than most, who would be going to bed without. Tito kicked off his shoes and joined Tommy in the kitchen.

His brother was in front of the stove, stirring a pot. He was a carbon copy of Tito, except for the fact that Tommy was much smaller and slimmer. That was courtesy of his lifetime of illness. But that was about to end soon. If Tito shopped smart, he would be able to use a small amount of the money that Georgio gave him to get a couple of nice outfits. Then Tito could stash the rest of it. With his next paycheck, he just might finally have enough to take Tommy to the doctor.

"It smells good," Tito said.

Tommy gave him a glib look. "It smells like it does every day in here during dinnertime."

"Well, it's better than nothing."

"You're always so optimistic. I'll bet those gangsters you work for don't have to live off this crap. They eat only the best and don't give a damn about the rest of us," Tommy said bitterly.

It was no big secret that Tommy hated the gang that ran their sector. Which was why he was so pissed off that Tito was working for them. But at the end of the day, it had been the only halfway decent job that Tito could get. He had no training in anything, no education, and he came from the slums. So it wasn't exactly like employers were lining up to beg him to work for them.

"It's money, Tommy. That's all that matters."

Tommy threw down the spoon in frustration. "They only hired you because you're expendable to them. Everybody knows that runners are easy pickings for rival gangs. Almost every day, there is another story about some runner who is killed, then butchered and sent back to the twins as some kind of message."

Tito felt a shiver go down his spine. What Tommy said was true. Just the other day, he'd been there when a box was delivered. Michael had opened it and found the body parts of one of his runners.

Instead of getting mad, the sick bastard had merely shrugged his shoulders and said, "Looks like we're going to have to find a new runner. I hate it when I have to take time out of my day to do that."

"I know it's dangerous," Tito told Tommy, "but I don't have any choice. We need to get the money to take you to the doctor. Plus I want to get us the hell out of this neighborhood."

"It's not worth it if you get yourself killed in the process."

"I'm careful, plus I'm a very fast runner. I won't let them catch me," Tito assured his brother.

"I still think you're stupid for taking that job."

"It's not as bad as you think. Plus, not all the brothers are as bad as you think. The younger one went with me to a particularly hard client. When we were finished, he even gave me some money so I could buy some better clothes."

"I don't see either of the twins doing that," Tommy scoffed.

"It wasn't one of the twins—it was their younger brother, Georgio."

Tommy let out a gasp. "You get that look off your face right now."

"What look?"

"The sappy one you get whenever you meet a guy that you think is sexy."

"I don't have that expression on my face," Tito countered.

"Yes, you do. You think Georgio is hot, admit it."

"No, I don't," Tito lied. "And even if I did, he would be way out of my league. Besides, he's probably not even gay. Everybody knows what kind of trouble somebody can get into for that."

Although that hadn't stopped the twins from leering at Tito as if it were lunchtime and he was that day's special. It'd gotten so bad that he'd done everything that he could to make sure that he was never alone in the twins' presence. The last thing he wanted was to have to put in some mandatory *overtime*. Now, if Georgio asked him to, Tito would jump at the chance. Even if it was a one-time experience. Tito was no fool—he knew there was never any hope that he and Georgio could form a real relationship. They came from two different worlds. If Georgio saw where Tito lived, the poor guy would probably run away in the opposite direction as fast as he could and never look back again.

No, Tito was doomed to live a sad and lonely life, even if he did manage to get them out of the slums. There was no way he could ever make love to a woman, and if paired up with another man, they would find their asses in jail before their first night together was over. Tito might as well give up and start collecting cats now.

Tommy frowned, as if he knew what Tito was thinking. "It really sucks to be us, doesn't it?"

Tito thought back to the guy who he'd seen beaten and bloodied in the twins' office earlier that day. "Trust me, things could be a worst."

"You must have already seen some pretty bad things at your job."

Tito gave a slight nod. "You could say that, but it's nothing I can't handle."

Tommy scooped out the rice and beans, then put the food on two chipped plates. He carried them over to the table then sat down. "Come on and eat. You must be starving."

"I am. I skipped lunch so I could take on extra jobs. The more deliveries you make, the more money they pay you."

"Does it ever bother you that your so-called deliveries are either threat letters for late payments or taking cash from merchants? Money that they have to pay to the twins if they want to run a business in this district."

Tito had trouble swallowing the food in his mouth because his throat had grown dry. "That may be true, but have those same merchants ever done anything to help us? No, they just turn a blind eye to the slums while we die and waste away. So I don't have any problem seeing them sweat it out for once."

"When did you become so bitter?" Tommy asked.

"The first time I heard you crying yourself to sleep, because you were hungry and we didn't have any food in the house."

Tommy gaped at him. "I had to have been like three at that time. That's a long time to hold a grudge."

"I know," Tito replied. "Some days, it's the only thing that keeps me going."

* * * *

As soon as Georgio had gone to his brothers' place and turned over the envelope of money, he left as quickly as he could. The last thing he wanted was to spend one more second in their company.

Luckily, they were too preoccupied with their weekly poker game to pay him much attention, so Georgio was able to get out of there without any words being exchanged. Georgio only wished that every encounter he had with his brothers were that easy. Maybe then Georgio wouldn't have an ulcer at the age of twenty-five.

Instead of going to his home, he went to Dirk's place. Since Dirk lived alone, he wouldn't have anybody to take care of him, and Georgio knew his friend would need some tending to after the brutal beating he'd taken.

Georgio went up the steps of Dirk's high-end house and let himself in with the key Dirk had given him long ago. As soon as he walked in, Georgio let out a curse. The place smelled like blood. There was even a crimson trail on the floor. Georgio followed it until he reached the living room.

Damn it. It was even worse than Georgio had imagined. Dirk lay on the couch, one leg up on the furniture, the other one on the floor. His face was unrecognizable, because it was such a mash of bruises and cuts. Some of the wounds were still bleeding, the thick liquid dribbling onto the cushion under his head.

What worried Georgio more was the blood that was coming from Dirk's stomach and leg. His once white shirt was now red, and there was a steady dripping coming from the hem of his pants.

"Shit," Georgio said as he rushed toward Dirk. "Are you even conscious?"

After a few heart gripping moments of silence, Dirk finally mumbled, "Yes, but I wish to God that I wasn't. I feel like I was beaten to hell and back again."

Georgio wondered if maybe Dirk had taken one too many blows to the head. "That's because you were beaten."

"Ah, that would explain why my ribs feel like they're in a million pieces. It would also explain why I feel like I'm about to cough up half a lung."

"Did you go to the doctor?" Georgio asked.

Dirk gave Georgio a glare, but it didn't quite come off as intimidating since the man's eyes were nearly swollen shut. "And just what would I tell the doctor? That I fell down a flight of stairs? Somehow, I don't think they would believe that."

Georgio rolled his eyes. "You could have told them the truth. Even the doctors are under my brothers' thumbs. They wouldn't have said a word to anybody."

"I just figured that the fewer people who knew, the better it would be for all of us."

"What if you have brain damage or a fracture?"

"It'll mend by itself, just like all the others have."

A wave of guilt rolled over Georgio. He knew damn well that one of the reasons the twins targeted Dirk so much was because they knew that he and Georgio were best friends. Georgio also had a sick feeling in his stomach that one day they would take things too far and end up killing Dirk. Georgio knew he had to find a way to protect Dirk, but damned if he knew how. It was near impossible to smuggle somebody out of a district, and that was the only way Georgio could think of to get Dirk away from his brothers.

"It's all my fault," Georgio said.

"No, it's not. How many times do I have to tell you to stop with all that drama and angst crap? Just help me clean up a bit, get me a beer and stay with me tonight to make sure I don't die in my sleep, and we'll be all good."

Georgio nodded, then got up. Going to Dirk's room, Georgio retrieved some fresh clothing for his friend, before going to the bathroom and wetting down several washcloths with warm water. He knew from past experience that the clothing was going to be stuck in some places, and it would help to let the clothes soak on the wounds before. Even then, it would still hurt like a son of a bitch when Georgio pulled the material free from Dirk's skin.

Georgio then grabbed the first aid kit that he had stashed at Dirk's place. Not only did it contain gauze, bandages and the usual stuff, but it also had some strong painkillers in it. There were some perks to being the younger brother of the ruling gangsters of the district, and for once, Georgio hadn't felt guilty about using them. Dirk was a good friend, and he didn't need or deserve to go through more pain than he had to.

After going back into the living room, Georgio carefully tended to Dirk's wounds. Even though Georgio was as gentle as he could be, his friend still winced several times as his clothing was pulled off.

Finally, Dirk was down to his boxers, and Georgio could see the full extent of the injuries to his friend.

Damn, it was easily the worst beating that Dirk had received. His entire body was one huge bruise. There were even some on his feet. Georgio had always hated his brothers, but at that moment, he wanted them dead. Those bastards had gone too far this time. Georgio had to do something to make their days of tyranny end.

But what could he do? He was the youngest son of the family, and they held a firm grip on their control. If Georgio were to take one step in the wrong direction and they found out, he knew for a fact his brothers would have no trouble taking him out.

Georgio let out a sigh. He had never felt so helpless in his life.

Chapter Four

Over the next few months, life fell into an easy pattern for Tito. He kept working as a runner for the twins, and his paychecks kept coming in. Things began to improve for him and Tommy, to the point that Tito was eventually able to take Tommy to the doctor. They diagnosed Tommy with asthma and gave him some medication to treat it. Tommy began to thrive, so much that it was amazing. Tito couldn't believe that a disease that had plagued Tommy all of his life could be cured by a simple inhaler and some pills. It was so stupid that it made Tito want to punch something. But when he looked over at Tommy and saw that his brother's coloring was normal for the first time in his life and that he could move around without wheezing, Tito's anger would fade. All that mattered was that Tommy was well now. Tito would just have to learn to let go of the past, as hard as it might be.

Tito was running one of his drops into the twins' office. As always, he looked around for Georgio. Not only did the man always have an encouraging smile for him, but they'd even had several conversations. Tito was amazed that Georgio wanted to spend any time with Tito, let alone take the effort to talk to him and get to know him.

During those encounters, Tito was shocked to find that not only did Georgio have a wicked sense of humor, but also that he was an outrageous flirt. It didn't bother Tito, though, like the way the twins did. Georgio did it in a light, fun way that actually had Tito laughing on more than one occasion.

When Tito looked around and only saw Georgio in the office, a heady thrill went through him. It was so rare that they had any periods where they were alone. Not that Tito was a fool. He knew that he was just a fun little diversion for Georgio, but Tito couldn't help but relish the attention he received from the gangster.

"Hey, there's my favorite runner," Georgio said.

"You just say that because all the other runners gush over your brothers," Tito countered.

He handed the envelope of money over to Georgio, who tossed it to the side casually. The move didn't surprise Tito. In the small amount of time that he'd come to know Georgio, he'd learned that Georgio had no interest in the family business. In fact, on more than one occasion, Tito had seen disgust on Georgio's face when his brothers ordered a beat down. It was clear that Georgio was the only one in the family who had been gifted with any form of empathy.

Georgio got up from behind the desk then walked up to Tito. Tito froze in shock. They were only inches apart, and he could feel the warmth of Georgio's body. It made Tito think of how it would feel if they were pressed together, without any barrier between them, not even clothes.

"You've been doing a very good job," Georgio said.

The compliment washed over Tito, giving him a heady thrill. "Thank you."

Georgio reached out and ran the back of his fingers over Tito's cheek, his touch making Tito shiver in delight. Tito was sure that he had to be dreaming because there was no way that Georgio, of all men, would be acting this way toward him. Tito was from the slums, he was a nobody, a shadow in Georgio's high-class world.

"Why don't we go into my office so we can have a little more privacy?" Georgio suggested.

"Are you serious?" Tito asked, his voice rising just a bit.

Georgio took a step back. "If you don't want to, that's okay. I'll understand, and I won't fire you or punish you in any way. I just thought from the way you'd been looking at and talking to me, that you were attracted to me."

Tito realized he was coming close to blowing the one thing he wanted more than anything in the world. He reached forward and grabbed Georgio's hand. "I am attracted to you. Very much so. I'd just never imagined that you would ever like me in return."

Georgio slowly shook his head. "Why would you ever think that?"

"Come on. You have to admit. I'm not exactly in your league. I was born and raised in the slums and I'm still there now. Even though I'm part of your gang, I'm lowest on the totem pole. So it's not like I'm bringing much to the table."

Georgio cupped Tito's face. "You are worth far more than you will ever know. I only wish that you could see yourself through my eyes. Now, let's go to my office."

He took Tito by the hand and led him to an office. While it was large and pretty opulent, it was still much smaller than the twins'. Tito was willing to bet that there wasn't a roll of plastic in the closet either. Georgio was too kind and gentle to ever sit there and take glory over watching somebody being beaten or killed in front of him.

Georgio spun Tito around so that they were facing each other — he then began to walk forward, forcing Tito to backtrack. They didn't stop moving until Tito was pinned in the corner of room. Only then did Georgio reach down and cup Tito's chin.

"I'm going to kiss you. Is that okay?" Georgio asked.

"Yes, I think I would like that very much."

Georgio dipped his head down and captured Tito's lips in a hot, demanding kiss. Tito gripped Georgio by the shoulders, then stood on tiptoe so he could return the kiss, his mind going wild with a flurry of thoughts. The one that hit him the most was *he wants me, he really wants me. Even if it's for this moment.*

Georgio made it clear that he was the one in charge, but he wasn't hurtful about it. He just had a dominating presence that made Tito want to submit. He didn't even complain when Georgio grabbed Tito by his hair and forced him to tilt his head back.

Georgio then tore his lips away from Tito's mouth and began to kiss and nip his way down Tito's throat. Tito let out a series of small moans. While he'd been with other men before, it'd always been quick hookups. Never before had any of his past lovers taken their time to linger and really pamper Tito. Now that he knew what he'd been missing, Tito felt cheated.

But then Georgio began to suck on one particular spot on Tito's neck, and suddenly, he didn't care about the past. All that mattered to Tito was the present and what Georgio was doing to him now. And damn it if it wasn't good.

When Georgio reached between them and cupped Tito's cock, Tito jumped in shock. Georgio let out a muffled laugh before he started to undo Tito's pants. Since Tito never wanted to waste what little money he had on something like underwear, Georgio immediately came into contact with Tito's hard cock.

"Oh, look what I've found," Georgio said in a near whisper.

He gave Tito's cock a slight squeeze before he dropped to his knees in front of Tito. Tito let out a small gasp, but before he could say anything, Georgio stuck his tongue out and ran it around the tip of Tito's cock.

A jolt of pleasure shot through Tito that was so intense he threw his head back, hitting the wall. Then when Georgio did it again, Tito thought for sure he was going to die from euphoria.

Just as Tito was sure things couldn't possibly get any better, Georgio opened his lips and took Tito's cock into his mouth. Tito tried to bite back his cry of pleasure, but it was useless. So he put his fist to his teeth to stifle the sound instead.

Georgio began to bob his head back and forth, starting up a steady yet not too fast rhythm. Before long, Tito found himself pumping his hips, eager to get deeper. Tito was both impressed and relieved when Georgio didn't gag. Then again, maybe it could just mean that Tito had a little cock. Which was kind of a bummer thought.

Georgio reached up with his free hand and began to massage Tito's balls. Oh God, that was just so unfair. How was Tito to hold back from coming when

Georgio did that? Tito was close to coming, too—the tingling sensation at the base of his spine told him that.

"Georgio, if you don't stop, I'm going to…"

Georgio's response was to give Tito's ball another hard squeeze. That shredded the last of Tito's control, and throwing back his head again, he let out a loud cry. His cock shot off stream after stream of cum. Georgio easily swallowed it down, not letting one drop slip from his mouth. The entire time, Tito ran his hands through Georgio's soft hair. Finally, Tito was done. Georgio stood and gave Tito another kiss before he reached down and tucked Tito's cock back into his pants.

Tito thought it was only fair that he reciprocate. So he began to drop to his knees, but Georgio stopped him. The move confused Tito, and he looked up at Georgio.

"Don't you want a blow job?"

Georgio gave a small laugh. "More than you can imagine. I just don't think we better risk being in here alone together for too long. I don't want people to get suspicious."

Tito palmed Georgio's hard cock. Even through the layers of his clothing, Tito could tell the gangster was hard. The poor guy had to be on the edge and hurting.

"It doesn't seem fair that I found some relief and you didn't," Tito said.

"Don't think I didn't enjoy what we did as much as you did. I've wanted to taste you since the moment I first saw you."

Tito felt a heat come over his face. "Really?"

"There're two things I never lie about, great sex and hot men."

Tito rolled his eyes. "I'm sure that's true."

"It is. Now go home. I'll see you in the morning." Georgio gave Tito a gentle slap on his ass.

For the first time ever, Tito found himself reluctant to leave his job. But the twins had returned, and Tito wanted to be as far away from them as possible. He really hated the way they looked at him. It just gave him the heebie-jeebies with a dash of ewww. Rushing past them so they wouldn't have a chance to say anything to him, Tito ran outside.

For once, he was happy to be greeted by the acrid, polluted Chicago air. For Tito, that meant freedom. But he wasn't a fool. He knew that one day he would be there alone and the twins would come in and find him. Then who the hell knew what would happen, but Tito had a sickening feeling that it wouldn't be good.

Tito raced home. Tommy had told him that morning that he wanted to take Tito someplace after work. Tito had tried to get more details out of Tommy, but his brother had been closemouthed and refused to tell him anything more. Tito swore that if his brother was dragging him to a dice game or something, he was going to strangle Tommy. Tito was too tired for that kind of shit.

As soon as he walked into the front door, his brother shoved a sandwich in his hand and said, "You're late. We have to hurry, or we're going to be late."

"Are you finally going to tell me where we're going?" Tito asked.

"We're going to a meeting."

"What kind of meeting?"

"For the resistance."

Tito was so shocked that he almost dropped his sandwich. "Are you fucking kidding me? You're going to get us both killed. If they find out that we're members or that we've even been near the resistance, they'll shoot us on the spot and feed us to their dogs. I mean that literally, too. I've seen them do it."

Tommy turned on his brother. "You're the one who is always saying how unfair things are. How it's wrong that only a small percentage of society is rich, while the rest of us live in squalor. How we're helpless to change things. Well, this is our chance to change things. Instead of just whining about it, put your money where your mouth is and do something. Yes, it may be dangerous, but if we don't fight back, then things are never going to change. Now, are you with me or not?"

Tito blinked a few times. "Well, after a speech like that, how could I not be? Damn, I never knew you had it in you."

Tommy grabbed Tito by the arm and said, "Let's get going. It's a little bit away from here, and we have to make sure we're not being tailed."

"I have to walk, eat my sandwich and make sure we're not being followed all at the same time? What do you think I am? A superhero?"

Tommy let out a sigh. "Just come on."

They walked outside. It had grown dark, and in their part of the neighborhood, there weren't any streetlights. So they were able to make it through there pretty quickly. Tito took that opportunity to eat. By the time they reached the city, he'd already finished with his food and was able to look around better to make sure they weren't being tracked.

Not that he really expected to be. Nobody really paid any attention to two young slum rats. But Tito knew that they couldn't be too careful. The last thing he wanted was to find himself kneeling on a piece of plastic in front of the twins' desk. They seemed to be walking forever before Tommy stopped at a door. It looked like nothing special. Just like the many others that led to various apartments in the city. If anything, Tito would call it weathered a bit. It used to be red, but now it was faded and peeling in places.

Tommy pounded out a series of knocks that were timed into a certain beat. Tito had to refrain himself from rolling his eyes. Seriously, did they have a secret knock? What was next? Special decoder rings?

After a moment, Tito could sense somebody looking at them through the peephole. Then the door opened. An elderly man stood on the other side. Surprisingly, he looked like he was one of the richer citizens. He even had his gray hair slicked back and his mustache waxed into fine points.

"Hurry, hurry. Get inside before somebody sees you," he urged.

Tito and Tommy rushed inside, and the door was closed. Tito glanced around so he could get his first impression of who was in this rebellion. Then his gaze fell on somebody on the far left, and his heart stopped. Never would he have believed that he would see that particularly man there.

"Georgio? What in the hell are you doing here?"

Chapter Five

Georgio couldn't believe his eyes. Never in a million years would he have imagined that he would see Tito of all people at the rebellion safe house. Yet there he stood, as cute as ever, right in the middle of a place that could very well get his perky little ass killed.

"What in the hell are you doing here?" Georgio demanded.

"I asked you first," Tito pointed out.

"I think it's pretty obvious. I'm not here to join the knitting club."

"Well, that's a bummer. I could have really used a new scarf for the winter. You know how cold it gets."

Georgio wanted to shake some sense into Tito. It really wasn't time for jokes. "Do you know what will happen if my brothers find you here?"

"Probably the same thing that will happen if they find you here, only it will be a lot worse for you. They'll tear you to pieces before they kill you. So why are you taking the risk?"

Georgio ran a hand through his hair. This was the only safe place where he could say what he was thinking. "Because I'm sick of the violence. Seeing people die all the time just because they don't have enough food to eat. I'm done with watching children beg on the street because their family doesn't have anywhere to live. Meanwhile my brothers have everything they want and then some, just because they're the best at killing. It's unfair and needs to be changed."

Tito stared at Georgio for a few moments as if he had grown another head or something before he finally said, "I feel the same way. The only reason I came to work for your brothers in the first place is because I was desperate for money. I hate them and everything they stand for. When I realized that you weren't the same way they were, I was so happy."

Georgio reached out and hooked an arm around Tito's waist. Pulling him in close, Georgio placed a soft kiss on Tito's head. How he wished he could keep Tito away from the danger. But if there was one thing he knew about Tito, it was how stubborn the man could be. If he was determined to be part of the resistance, there was no way that Georgio was going to talk him out of it.

"Just promise me you'll be careful. You've come to mean a lot to me, and it would destroy me if something were to happen to you," Georgio said.

"Back at ya," Tito replied.

"We better go find a seat. The meeting is about to start."

They went in and sat down next to Dirk. Tito studied Dirk a moment before he said, "Weren't you the guy who was being beaten up by the twins that one day I came in with a delivery?"

Dirk gave Tito a crooked smile. "Thanks for the reminder, but yes, I was."

A pink hue covered Tito's face. "I'm sorry. I didn't mean to bring up any bad memories or anything."

"That's okay. I was just giving you a hard time. You must be the Tito that Georgio talks about all the time."

"Leave it," Georgio growled.

"Seriously, he never stops talking about you. Although now that I've finally got a good look at you, I can see why."

Georgio was going to strangle his friend if he didn't shut his mouth up. Sure, he had mentioned Tito to him a time or ten, but he didn't have to tell Tito about it. Damn, Tito was going to think that Georgio was some sicko stalker or something.

Tommy leaned forward. "Don't worry, Tito talks about Georgio all the time, too. It's gotten to the point where I just turn it into white noise and nod."

Tito turned bright red. "There are some things that we keep to ourselves."

Thankfully, before things could go any further, Wilkenson, the elderly man who ran the resistance, came forward and called a start to the meeting.

"Welcome to everyone who was brave enough to come tonight. I know what a big risk it was for all of you. A situation has come to our attention, and it is of the upmost importance."

Georgio leaned forward in his seat. He had a feeling that something big was going to happen to their resistance, and that things may never be the same again. Without caring who saw, he reached out and grabbed Tito's hand, holding it tightly.

Wilkenson continued, "We have come into possession of USB drives that hold very sensitive material to the resistance. By this, I mean something that could finally bring down all the gangs in the districts for good. We need to be able to pass it on to the next district, but it's not going to be easy. We've looked at all possible options, and the only way we'll be able to do it is at the railroad crossing on Tenth Street. There is a gap in the fences there, and if somebody is brave enough to do it, they can jump from the platform to the train from the other district. They have already promised us that there will be a contact person there to meet them."

Georgio raised his hand. "How will we get our person back to our district?"

"We won't. Whoever volunteers will be stuck in the neighboring district until our plan works and we are victorious."

"But what about their papers and identification? Won't they be caught?" Georgio asked.

"We have a good forger who is part of the resistance. He will be able to make a copy of papers that should be passable."

"*Should* be passable?"

Wilkenson let out a sigh. "There are no sure things in this kind of war. We all know that."

"I'll do it," Dirk spoke up.

Shocked, Georgio turned to his friend. "Are you out of your mind? Do you have any idea how dangerous this mission is?"

Dirk gave him a bland look. "Yeah, I was listening to the speech, just like you. But if I stay here, it will only be a matter of time before your brothers kill me. We both know that."

Georgio wanted to argue that point. To offer some words of comfort. To say something. But in the end, he had to admit to himself that Dirk was right. The last thing Georgio wanted was to see his friend die. This was one of the ways that they could keep him safe, short of putting him in a safe house and keeping him there for God knows how long. Dirk would be alone then, and his friend was the type that needed to interact with others or else he would go crazy.

"Fine, but I want to at least walk you to the railroad ramp. I need to know that you made it to the train safe," Georgio said.

"Okay," Dirk said before turning to Wilkenson and asking, "When do I leave?"

"It has to be right now, I'm afraid. You won't have any time to go back to your place to pack. I was assured by my contacts that they would provide everything for you and take care of your needs. The train arrives in fifteen minutes."

Dirk and Georgio stood. That didn't leave them much time. They would have to run to get there, all the while making sure that they weren't being followed. At least once they left the main part of the city they would have the cover of darkness on their side.

Georgio turned and gave Tito a blistering kiss. "I'll be back soon."

"Do you promise?" Tito asked in a shaky voice.

"Yes, I do. Especially when I have something so special waiting for me."

He then turned and walked away, Dirk at his side. They carefully peered out of the door, making sure nobody was looking before they slid outside. Then walking quickly, yet casually, they began to make their way to Tenth Street.

Once they reached the edge of the city, it grew dark, so Georgio and Dirk were able to run. In the distance, they could hear the horn from the train. Georgio picked up his pace. If they didn't get to the platform in time, they were going to miss the opportunity for them to pass over the flash drive. They couldn't let that happen.

When the platform came into view, Georgio let out a sigh of relief. Yet at the same time, he felt sad because he knew that this could be his last moments with his friend. It felt so bittersweet that Georgio's heart clenched a bit. He only hoped that Dirk was going into a better situation than the one he was running from.

They climbed up onto the platform just as the train was approaching. The whoosh of the train made Georgio's hair blow, and he wondered just how safe it was for Dirk to try to jump into one of the boxcars. The last thing he wanted was to see his friend end up splattered on the side of a train. What a way to go out—death by train.

"How are we going to know which one you're supposed to jump into?" Georgio asked.

"I'm guessing it's that one."

Dirk pointed to a red car. The door was open, and a hand was out and waving. Georgio felt his heart beat faster and faster the closer the train got to them.

Dirk turned to Georgio. "This is goodbye for now, but not forever. I know we will eventually see each other again."

Before Georgio could even reply, Dirk patted his pocket that held the USB drives, then leaped off the platform. For one breathtaking moment, Georgio didn't think that Dirk was going to make it, but at the very last moment, his friend cleared the door and made it inside the boxcar.

Georgio stood there, his heart still pounding as he watched the train disappear into the night. It was done. They had successfully passed over the information. While Georgio should be happy, a part of him couldn't help being sad. Now he didn't know if he would ever see Dirk again. Which would be odd since Dirk had been a part of Georgio's life for as long as he could remember.

Georgio finally turned around and made his way back to the rebellion headquarters. As soon as he walked in, Tito ran across the room and threw himself into Georgio's arms. Georgio held him for a moment, relishing Tito's smell. Georgio was glad to know that even though he had lost his friend, he still had Tito, and that mattered the most to him. The runner had managed to wiggle his way into Georgio's heart, and there was no way that Georgio was ever going to let him go.

"I'm so happy that you made it back. I was worried about you," Tito said.

"Didn't I promise you that I would return?" Georgio asked.

"Yes."

"I don't ever break a promise. You'll learn that soon enough."

Georgio went down for a kiss. Suddenly, the front door crashed open, and the twins and the enforcers rushed into the room, guns blazing. Bullets began to fly around everywhere. Many of them hitting rebels, causing them to fall to the ground.

Georgio grabbed Tito by the waist and brought him down, shielding him with his own body. Tito let out a small grunt as they fell, but as far as Georgio could tell, Tito was okay. The floor was covered with blood, the sticky liquid soaking into their clothing.

Soon the members of the rebellion got out their own weapons and began to fire back. That caused the gangsters to retreat a bit so they were crowded in the small entryway that led to the main room. Georgio even got into the action, getting off Tito and firing back at the gangsters. He didn't even care that he was shooting at his own brothers. All that mattered was that Tito was safe and that they got out of the house alive.

Eventually, the rebellion group outgunned the gangsters. Not that Georgio was surprised. His brothers were always cocky, and they hadn't brought enough men with them to win the fight. Hopefully, one day that would be their downfall.

Georgio edged out from behind the row of chairs he'd taken cover at and squeezed off a shot. When he heard Michael yell in pain and saw a splash of crimson show up on his brother's left shoulder, Georgio only felt a slight twinge of guilt. After seeing all the pain and destruction Michael had caused in the past, it made it hard for Georgio to feel too bad for him.

"Retreat!" Michael finally called.

It was then that Georgio realized that only the twins and a few of the enforcers remained, most of whom were wounded. A few of them looked so bad it would be a miracle if they made it back to the twins' headquarters.

Somebody from the rebellion opened the back door of the house. "Everybody get out now!"

Georgio didn't hesitate a second. He hauled Tito to his feet, looked behind him to make sure that Tommy was following, then booked the hell out of there. Once they were outside, they found themselves in a small alley. A manhole cover had been taken out, and members of the rebellion were going down into it, one by one.

"Where are we going?" Georgio asked.

"To our secondary safe house. Then we're going to have to put you into deep hiding. There is no way that your brothers didn't recognize you. They will put a huge-ass bounty on your head," Rory, one of the top members of the rebellion, said.

"I'll only go if Tito and Tommy go with me. Tito worked as a runner for them so they'll be after him, too," Georgio argued.

Rory looked over at Tito, before he gave a firm nod. "We'll take care of them, too. But we need to hurry and get out of here before your brothers return and bring reinforcements."

With a nod of his own, Georgio began to climb down into the manhole. He only hoped that he and Tito would get out of the war alive.

Chapter Six

The walk through the sewers was worse than Georgio could have ever imagined. The water went up past their ankles. They could hardly see, and for that, Georgio was grateful. Things were floating past him and bumping into his legs, and he did not want to know what they were.

Off to each side, he could hear the scurrying and scratching of rats. Georgio let out a shudder as he thought about how many of the creatures must be in the tunnels with them. Their beady little eyes staring at them. Georgio almost felt as if the furry, dirty creatures were sizing them up and getting ready to attack. Just the thought of being bitten by those things made him feel sick to his stomach.

The worst thing had to be the smell, though. It was beyond rancid. So much so that it burned the inside of Georgio's nostrils. He tried to bring his handkerchief up to his nose, in hopes of masking some of the scent, but it was useless. Georgio felt that he could be wearing a gas mask and the stench would still permeate through it.

Behind him, he could hear Tommy wheezing. Georgio began to worry about the young man. Tito had told Georgio about Tommy's medical diagnosis. This smell had to be playing hell on the kid's asthma. He was using his inhaler, but it didn't seem to be helping much. Georgio knew that they had to get Tommy out of there as soon as possible.

"How much longer?" Georgio asked Rory.

"Just a bit. We have to drop the others off at our next safe house. Then we have to walk a little while longer to take you three to your place," Rory replied.

"Tommy isn't doing so well," Georgio pointed out.

Rory shot a worried look over his shoulder. "Yeah, I noticed that, too. I'm trying my best to get you there as fast as I can. I promise you."

They walked a bit farther, and the rest of the group, save for Rory, Georgio, Tito and Tommy, climbed up a ladder. Georgio felt a little sense of relief because he knew that they had reached one milestone and that they only had a little while longer to go until they reached their location.

"It should only be about fifteen minutes longer. Can you handle that, Tommy?" Rory asked.

Tommy nodded his head before letting out a series of hacking coughs. Georgio exchanged worried looks with Tito, but they continued to walk on. They all knew that they wouldn't be completely safe until they made it to their new location. Georgio was no fool. He was well aware that his brothers already had their enforcers out, looking for him and Tito.

Finally, after what seemed like forever, Rory stopped at a ladder. "This is our location."

* * * *

Georgio rubbed the towel over his wet head. He had just taken the longest shower in his life, and it was nice to finally feel clean. Tito was off in one of the house's other bathrooms taking a shower himself. As for Tommy, they had let him wash first, and he was already sleeping in one of the three bedrooms.

Their new home was nice. It wasn't opulent like Georgio's last home, but it was small and comfy. He found that he liked that better. Plus it was far outside of the city, so they had fresh air to breathe, which Georgio knew would do wonders for Tommy's asthma.

Georgio was only dressed in his robe, but he didn't plan on changing out of it anytime soon. It was nice to be free from the confines of his suit for once. In fact, if he never had to put one on again, he could die a very happy man.

There was a rustle of movement at his door, and he looked over. What he saw took his breath away. Tito was standing there wearing nothing but a towel wrapped around his waist. Beads of water still clung to his slightly golden skin, and his hair was wet and slicked back.

While he might be on the thinner side, that didn't mean he was without a manly body. Defined pecs and an impressive eight-pack called to Georgio. Even his calves were perfectly shaped, no doubt from all those hours of running through the Chicago streets delivering packages.

"You know, they have robes for us on the back of the door in the bathroom," Georgio said.

"I know, but I thought you would like it better if you had easy access to me."

Desire rushed through Georgio. "Are you trying to tell me what I think you are?"

Tito cocked an eyebrow. "Do I have to get a neon sign? I've been waiting for you to fuck me for ages. Now we finally have the time. Unless you don't want to."

Not want to? Is Tito out of his mind?

Georgio had wanted the man from day one. Now that he had him within his grasp, nothing short of a bombing would stop him from taking him.

"Do you have any lube?" Georgio asked, his voice raspy with need.

Tito held up a bottle of lotion. "Sorry, we'll have to make do with this. At least it's not rose scented or anything, so we won't smell like old ladies when we're done."

Georgio crooked his finger. "Well, then come here so we can get started."

Tito let the towel drop so he was completely nude. His cock was already hard and curled up toward his taut belly. Even from across the room, Georgio could see a pearl of pre-cum at the head. Georgio licked his lips, remembering just how good Tito had tasted when Georgio had given him the blow job not so long ago. How Georgio would love to have another sample of that treat.

But that would have to wait for another time because this time Georgio planned on Tito coming when Georgio was inside him. No other situation would do. The time had come for Georgio to fully claim Tito. They had waited long enough, been through so much, that they deserved this one reward.

Georgio took his robe off. Tito let out a little gasp, but going by the smile on his face, Georgio could tell that Tito was pleased. Tito then began to walk toward Georgio. Georgio tracked Tito the entire way, loving how Tito moved. It was so damned sexy that Georgio was tempted to come right then. He could hardly believe that this little fireball belonged to him and him alone.

Once Tito got close enough, Georgio reached out and grabbed him, roughly pulling Tito closer. The skin-on-skin contact was the best thing Georgio had ever felt. Ramping it up a bit, he began to kiss Tito on the neck, at the same time running his fingers up and down Tito's back. Georgio let out a small smile when he felt Tito shiver in response.

Georgio walked backwards, leading them to the bed. Once they got there, Georgio spun them around and allowed them to fall, so Tito was on the bottom. Georgio then scooted them up a bit so they were fully on the bed.

"Perfect," Georgio said as he gazed down at Tito. "I finally have you just where I want you."

Georgio then began to kiss his way down Tito's body. When he got to Tito's nipples, Georgio gave them a lot of attention. Tito cried out, his hands going to Georgio's hair. Happy to find one of Tito's erogenous points, Georgio began to lick, nip and suck at Tito's nipples, making sure to give each one equal attention.

Tito began to hump Georgio's leg, but Georgio put an end to that. He reached down and grabbed Tito by the hip and stilled him. Tito let out a cry of protest, but Georgio just answered with a wicked laugh.

"Don't worry, you'll come. Just not yet. I want to have a lot more fun with you first," Georgio said.

"Damn it, you're driving me crazy, here," Tito protested.

"That's half the fun."

Tito let out a groan that soon turned into a gasp of pleasure when Georgio began sucking on his nipples again.

Georgio did it a few more moments before he gave his next order, "Turn over on your back."

Tito obeyed, even though it had to be a bit uncomfortable since it pinned his hard cock between his body and the mattress. Once Tito was there, Georgio sat back on his heels and began to run his hands over the rounded globes of Tito's ass. After doing that a few moments, he separated the halves and sought out Tito's hole.

Sticking his tongue out, Georgio traced a circle around the rim of Tito's opening. Tito almost reared off the bed and released a cry of pleasure. Georgio put a hand on the small of Tito's back to steady him and began to lick and nip at Tito hole.

"Oh my God, nobody has ever done this to me before," Tito said.

"Do you want me to stop?" Georgio asked.

"Hell no! If you do, I'll shoot you with your own gun."

Georgio had to admit to himself, he was proud that Tito was enjoying himself so much. Georgio speared his tongue inside Tito's hole. Tito wailed, his whole body shaking with pleasure. Georgio didn't stop until Tito was a limp, sobbing mess who was begging to be fucked.

Lifting his head, Georgio grabbed the bottle of lotion. Squeezing a generous amount onto the palm of his hand, Georgio slicked up one finger. With great care, he pushed it inside Tito. Tito didn't protest at all. In fact, he let out a sigh of relief as if he'd been waiting forever for this moment.

Georgio worked his finger in and out for a while before he added another one. Tito gave a small grunt, and for a moment, Georgio thought he'd hurt Tito. But then Tito began to rock back against Georgio's hand, and Georgio knew that Tito was getting into it.

By the time Georgio added a third finger, a sheen of sweat had broken out over Tito's body. It made his golden skin look all the more beautiful. Georgio knew then that he couldn't wait any longer—he had to get inside Tito.

Tito must have sensed it too because he got up on all fours and tilted his ass up. If that wasn't a fuck me invitation, then Georgio was missing some serious cues. He took out his fingers and replaced them with his cock.

Taking a deep breath, he slowly pushed into Tito. Damn, he was tight. So much so that Georgio almost lost it right then and there. But he was a man of self-control so he was able to hold back. It wasn't until he felt Tito relax around him that Georgio began to move.

Once he got started, he couldn't keep the slow, lazy pace that he wanted. Now that he was finally inside Tito, Georgio's previous self-control shredded into a million pieces. He grabbed Tito by the hips and began to pound into the man as hard as he could.

Tito wasn't complaining, though. If anything, he was urging Georgio on. He kept yelling out a string of dirty phrases that would have made a hooker blush. At the same time, he began to thrust back against Georgio, meeting him stroke for stroke.

Wanting his lover to find even more pleasure, Georgio reached down and stroked Tito's cock. It was already so wet with pre-cum that Georgio didn't have to worry about lubrication.

Tito finally cried out before he came, his cock shooting long streams of cum, covering both Georgio's hand and the bedding underneath them. When he did, his ass clamped down on Georgio's dick. That was enough to throw Georgio over the edge. Tossing his head back, he yelled out Tito's name as he found his own orgasm, his cock releasing wave after wave of hot cum into Tito's ass.

Once Georgio was finished, he pulled out, then rolled to the side of the bed so he didn't squash Tito. As for Tito, he had a huge smile of satisfaction on his face.

"So I gather that I pleased you?" Georgio asked.

"That and then some."

Georgio pulled Tito close to him. After a few moments, he could feel his lover's breathing grow even as he fell asleep. Georgio realized that he'd never been happier in his life. Sure, he might be running for his very survival, but he was with Tito and they were safe, for now.

Plus Georgio had faith in the rebellion. They would win in the end, and then Tito and Georgio would truly be free. But until then, Georgio was happy to wait, so long as he had Tito at his side.

GANGING UP ON LOVE

Amber Kell

Dedication

To romance lovers everywhere!

Chapter One

Dirk leaped for the train car. His foot caught the edge of the rail. Threatened with tumbling onto the moving track, he threw his body forward, slamming into the hard metal surface.

Groaning, he flopped onto his back.

"I see you haven't gotten any more graceful since I last saw you," a familiar voice spoke above him.

Dirk blinked to clear his vision. "Massy?"

His sister stood over him, a sly smile on her face. "Hello, brother dear." She held her pose for only a minute before she crouched down to his level and wrapped him in her arms. "I've missed you."

"Oh God, you're safe." He hugged her tight.

The fears he'd been harboring for the past few months eased. He'd worried she'd been killed by the mob. The White Widow ran Ward Four and from what he'd heard, she made the psycho twins in Ward Three seem like sweet cherubs. As the only female gang leader in Chicago, she ruled the ward through intimidation and outright bribes. What she couldn't get through threats she tossed money at, and she had

171

a lot to throw. Rumors flew that she'd killed off her husband to get control of the mob. She always wore white and bleached her hair to match. The sight of a white limo driving anywhere in Ward Four incited instant fear.

Dirk hugged Massy tight. Her bones were more prominent than they had been the last time he'd seen her.

They'd been close as children and even though they'd gone different paths as adults, he still had fond memories of chasing her through the city streets in games of tag while pickpocketing strangers. Even then, they'd had to earn money for the gangs.

She pushed futilely against him until he let her go. "I have to breathe."

"You always were such a picky thing," Dirk joked. He examined her carefully. She did look thinner but the smile on her face was genuine. "I missed you, Massy. Why didn't you tell me what you were up to?"

"Because your closest friend is the brother of mob bosses."

"You didn't trust me not to tell Georgio?" Hurt stabbed at him. He'd searched for her and had worried incessantly that she might be dead, and she'd held back because she doubted his loyalty? "When have I ever betrayed you? You didn't even leave me a note."

Regret flickered across her face. "I'm sorry. I just had to get out of there. I didn't think you'd say anything on purpose but if they tortured you then you wouldn't be able to tell them anything."

"Well, that worked." Dirk let bitterness fill his voice. "They almost beat me to death and I didn't tell them anything...just like I wouldn't have if I *had* known. These are from them!" He pointed out the bruises on his face. They'd blossomed into some truly brilliant colors.

He turned to look out the boxcar door, unwilling to meet his sister's eyes. Fury burned through him. He'd helped raise her after their parents had been murdered but she hadn't trusted him with her life. She'd always been independent and stubborn—bordering on selfish—but he'd thought they at least had trust between them.

"Dirk…" She put a hand on his shoulder.

He stood up, letting her hand fall away. "What?"

"I-I'm sorry. I came for you now, if that means anything."

"You didn't know who was coming." Dirk clenched his jaw to hold back the angry, hateful words teasing at the tip of his tongue. Sentences he'd never be able to take back once they hit the air were barely held in by his pressed lips.

"I did," Massy vowed. "They gave me enough hints that I knew who would come. I volunteered to be the contact. Leon didn't want me to come. He didn't think I was ready for such a big job."

"Who's Leon?" He turned to face his sister, reluctant to hear the answer to his question. She had probably married and was preparing to start a family since she'd abandoned him. It was like he didn't know her anymore.

Massy grinned. "He's the leader of the resistance in Ward Four. He's the one who got me transported safely and re-established. He'll do the same for you."

"Great. But what is he to you?" He didn't miss how she'd avoided that question.

A pink flush stole across her cheeks. Dirk dreaded her answer.

"Nothing yet."

Dirk sighed. "Does he know you like him?" Often the object of her affections was never aware of her existence. She'd been a gangly, plain child growing up, but it seemed that wasn't a problem any longer. She'd grown from a bothersome girl into a beautiful woman, even if she looked a little thin.

Massy shrugged. "He's warming up to me."

"As long as he doesn't get too warm without a wedding ring."

Dirk hated it when she arched an eyebrow at him. "What about you?"

"What about me?"

"Any signs of matrimony in your future?"

Dirk folded his arms over his chest. "In case you missed it, we are heading toward a revolution. When would I have a chance for romance?" Not to mention his choice wouldn't exactly be considered a good thing. He hoped things worked out for Georgio and Tito. The joy in Georgio's eyes when he saw Tito gave Dirk hope there might be someone out there for him. He just wasn't ready to find him yet.

Massy spoke and snapped him out of his reverie. "We get off at the next station. I'll tell you when to jump." She boldly slid the door back open to watch the scenery as it passed by.

"Why did you leave?" The words slipped out before he could stop them. Damn, he sounded needy, but he'd been wondering this entire time what had been the thing that had finally broken her.

Massy frowned. "They said if I didn't leave, they were going to kill you."

He froze. He hadn't been expecting that. "Who said that?"

"The twins. They said I was causing too much trouble."

A bitter laugh burst from him. "They almost beat me to death, claiming they needed your location."

Massy twirled a piece of hair around her index finger. "They were covering their tracks."

Dirk looked away, unable to handle the lies that had twisted through his life. The scenery blurred together—or maybe that was from his tears. Exhaustion pulled at him. When had he lost the path to a simpler life? All he wanted was a safe place to live and a solid man by his side.

Massy patted him on the back. He hadn't shared his innermost desires even to his sister. He couldn't handle it if his last remaining relative turned her back on him.

"Do you really think this information you have can be the key to bringing them all down?"

Dirk sighed. "Maybe. Or it could be a futile attempt that will end in our death."

He didn't know exactly what was on the drives. He'd only promised to bring them. Nothing good ever came from being a well-informed messenger.

"I see time hasn't made you more optimistic," Massy teased.

When had he last been optimistic? He searched his past but he couldn't remember. He'd worked so hard, scraping and bowing to the psychotic twins, that somewhere along the way he'd lost any hope or joy from life.

"What's it like in Four?"

Massy came to stand beside him—shoulder to shoulder they watched the underground tunnel swoop past. "A lot like the others, I imagine. Not as much fighting. There are actual pockets where the gangs aren't as intense. It's one of the better wards.

The White Widow keeps most of the lower gangs in check."

She said the words as if trying to convince herself. In truth, there were no good wards. There were bad or truly terrible ones, with subtle variances in between. Dirk had no belief in the police patrolling the streets or doing anything to hold back the gangs.

"I guess I'm stuck here now." One ward was as good as another, as far as Dirk could tell.

Massy gripped his arm. "If you hate it here, I'll have papers made up to get you out."

"Thanks, Massy." He didn't doubt she'd keep her word, but going from ward to ward was a dangerous proposition. Doing it even once could attract the wrong kind of attention.

The train began to slow, sliding out of the tunnel and back to the surface.

"Count to five then jump."

Dirk crept closer to the edge until the tips of his shoes lined up to the edge of the car. Silently, he counted backwards.

Five.

Four.

Three.

Two.

The crack of a gunshot echoed just as he leaped from the moving train. He landed hard on the asphalt, his jaw snapping together in a clack of teeth.

"Run!" Massy yanked on his arm and shoved him to the right. Trusting her to guide him, Dirk ran in the direction she indicated.

They fled through the rows of cars parked there for train passengers leaving on their journeys or coming to pick up friends. By getting off early, they had bypassed security. Apparently, the guards hadn't overlooked them. Another shot landed far too close as Massy ran toward a warehouse. A bullet pinged against the metal wall near Dirk's head. He hoped that wouldn't be the last sound he heard. The door swung open beneath Massy's tug. They ran inside and slammed the door after them. A series of bullets hit the door.

"Where to now?"

"Don't panic, brother. I wouldn't have led you astray," Massy promised.

Dirk nodded, even though he knew no such thing. The sister he'd thought he understood wouldn't have left town without word either.

The warehouse was completely empty. Dirk held back the curse aching to burst out. Yelling at his sister would do neither of them any good.

"Come. This way." She ran to the back of the warehouse and popped open a hidden latch in the cement floor. "Down here."

Despite his misgivings, he followed her down the shaky metal ladder, yanking the door down after him. Massy grabbed a lantern from a hook and pulled matches from her pocket to light the wick. Dirk hoped she hadn't started smoking again. It had taken her months to quit the last time.

The dim glow only brightened the immediate area around them enough that Dirk could see that the tunnel extended into further darkness.

"This goes beneath the entire city. We can reach headquarters from here."

"What about the door. Won't they find it?"

"They haven't so far."

Dirk hoped providence stayed on their side, because he didn't want to be trapped in the tunnel if a guard started shooting. There weren't exactly a lot of places to hide.

How long they stumbled along the dimly lit path Dirk didn't know. He'd forgotten to wind his watch in his rush out of town. He'd have to correct that as soon as he could. He hated feeling disconnected to the day.

"We're almost there." Massy pointed to a glowing outline up ahead.

A door.

"Great." Dirk let out the sigh he'd been holding inside.

The closer they came, the more details Dirk could make out, not the least of which was the lack of a knob or latch or any way to open the door.

Massy marched up to it and knocked a complicate series of raps Dirk knew he wouldn't be able remember, even if he tried.

After a few minutes of stomach churning silence, a series of clacks indicated locks were being unfastened. With a well-oiled slide, a crack appeared, just wide enough for them to slip through.

On his own, Dirk might've run the other way and taken a chance with the armed guards.

Massy didn't hesitate. She rushed inside. As soon as Dirk cleared the doorway, it slammed shut behind him. A dark-skinned man with startling green eyes examined him closely before refastening the locks.

"Benton, this is my brother Dirk. Is Leon around?"

Benton took his time ensuring the door was completely sealed before turning to Massy. "He's where he usually is."

Not exactly a ringing endorsement but Benton didn't strike Dirk as a wordy kind of fellow.

"Good. Follow me, Dirk."

Without anything else to do, Dirk trotted after his sister like a properly trained lapdog.

Chapter Two

Dirk nodded to the clusters of people gathered in small groups along the corridor. Massy didn't stop to acknowledge anyone. She shoved her way through and dragged Dirk after her. Somewhere along the way, she'd latched onto his wrist and no amount of tugging broke her iron hold.

"I can walk on my own," Dirk protested.

"Maybe, but this way I know you won't get lost. Too many girls down here grab onto newcomers. I don't want you to get trapped because you're too polite to brush them away."

Dirk searched his mind for a time when he'd been too polite for anything, but a particular instance didn't pop into his head.

He continued to stumble after Massy and was about to jerk her to a halt when they reached another door. This one she didn't bother knocking on. Instead, she shoved it open.

A man with dark hair and pale, almost colorless skin peeked around the corner.

"Jimmy, let us in. I brought the messenger."

Dirk remained silent. This was Massy's world. She knew the best way to introduce him to the group.

"Come inside." Jimmy waved them in.

Dirk was now more curious than ever before. He'd been told over the years that the resistance was composed of only a few people causing trouble. From what he'd seen so far, it was a lot more than just a handful of rebels. If there was a spot like this in each city, it wasn't completely impossible that they would reach their goals.

The room consisted of a wide wooden desk covered in maps and ledgers. A small computer sat on one side. Four men occupied the tiny space, but it was the one behind the desk that drew Dirk's attention. Black hair, probably once kept in a crisp cut, now fell in overgrown layers and drew attention to a warm pair of brown eyes. Their intensity was not dulled a bit by the set of wire-rimmed spectacles perched on his nose. Dirk had always liked the studious type.

He held back the whimper struggling to get out, when the handsome man smiled.

Gorgeous.

Dirk's mind went blank and he struggled to string two thoughts together.

"Leon, this is the messenger...my brother Dirk. He has some information to give you."

Leon stood. He took off his glasses and dropped them on the desk. Dirk held back the objection hovering on his lips. Leon should be forced to wear glasses all the time purely for the sexiness factor.

"What do you have?"

Dirk pulled the USB cufflinks out of his pocket and handed them over. "I was told these have information that could bring down the mob families. I don't know what it is."

He always made sure everyone knew the messenger was kept unaware. That had saved him more than once in his life when he'd first started out.

Their fingers touched when Leon accepted the drives. A zap of energy crackled between them. Dirk sucked in his breath. He'd been attracted to men before. This went beyond gentle attraction.

Heat flashed in Leon's eyes but he didn't comment and Dirk didn't expect him to. Lusting after a man could get him killed if his team suspected his inclinations. Some would be all right with it, but others would use it as a reason to take over and an excuse to end his life in a dark alley.

"Thank you, Dirk. I'll look these over. Massy, show your brother around but keep him near. I want to be able to find him if I have any questions. I'll have his papers done soon."

"You're welcome, but I doubt I'll have any answers. There wasn't time for a full debriefing. I had to get out of town before the twins killed me and every other part of the resistance."

"Understood." Leon's mouth tightened. Dirk expected him to say more but Leon only waved them out.

Massy dragged him after her. Once they were clear of the doorway, he yanked free. "I don't need you pulling me around. I can walk on my own."

"I didn't know if I needed to get you out of there before you started humping Leon." Her eyes flashed her displeasure.

Dirk snorted. "He's a gorgeous man."

He wouldn't lie. Massy might not approve of his inclinations now that she knew, but he didn't care. He hoped she'd keep the information to herself. From the little research he was able to do before he'd left, he'd learned Ward Four had a reputation for being the most overzealous in their oppression of gays. Keeping his eye on the local police could be another challenge.

"He's mine," she snarled. "I didn't rescue you only to let you have the guy I want."

"You have nothing to worry about. I doubt he's going to fall all over some guy he just met." Dirk kept his voice low, not wanting to draw attention to their conversation.

Massy sighed, abruptly losing her anger. "I just don't want you to get stabbed in a dark alley because they think you're corrupting our leader. I saw how he looked at you. He's interested."

Her defeated tone had Dirk gripping her shoulders. "It doesn't matter, because you know he's not going to pursue me."

"You don't know that."

Dirk's bitter laugh came out louder than he'd anticipated. "I can pretty much guarantee it."

"Come on. I'll show you where you can stay." She squeezed him, a quick, awkward sideways hug, before walking away.

Her mercurial moods always kept him off-balanced. He'd often wondered if maybe he needed to get her some sort of medication. Right now he couldn't worry about her. Massy was old enough to make her own choices.

He followed her through more twists and turns. Eventually she led him up a set of metal stairs.

The door at the top opened into a wood paneled hallway. "This is an apartment building we've taken over. There is an available one on the third floor." She pulled a set of keys out of her pocket and headed for a metal-caged elevator. "Leon put me in charge of housing a few days ago. I think it was to keep me out of trouble."

He couldn't fault Leon's logic. Sweat beaded Dirk's forehead as he examined the flimsy conveyance. "Are there stairs we can take?"

"Oh, right. Sorry." She swerved right and opened a discreet door marked 'Exit'.

"Thanks." Dirk knew he should've outgrown that phobia, but some childhood traumas were difficult to break. Memories of hours trapped in an elevator after a power outage still haunted him.

"No problem. Don't tell the others, though. These guys are always looking for weaknesses."

"I won't." Dirk could ride in an elevator when absolutely necessary, but it took all his fortitude and a bit of his sanity away with it. He didn't have to waste his energy impressing his sister.

They climbed the stairs to the third floor. Massy opened the door to the landing then led him down a shabby hall. The carpet was worn and faded and the paint needed a new coat but it didn't have any of the musty smells he expected from an older building.

"We've slowly been renovating, but it takes a lot of time and money." Massy flashed him an apologetic smile, as if it were her fault the building wasn't up to his standards.

Dirk shrugged. "Right now I'm too happy to be alive to be that concerned about where I'm staying."

It might be a huge step down from the luxurious place he'd left behind but he still had his life and most of his dignity. Right now he was pretty damn excited not to have been shot dead in an alley somewhere. She stopped in front of an apartment marked '303' and unlocked the door. Pushing the door open, she waved him inside. "Here it is."

Despite his words, a bit of trepidation filled him as he stepped through the door.

"Oh."

The floor of the apartment was covered in highly polished wood. The walls were painted a fresh coat of white and the furniture appeared, if not new, in gently used condition.

"It's one of the first we renovated."

"I don't have much money right now…" Dirk began. Once he got his new identification, he'd create a bank account, run his money through a third party cleaner then take out his funds. Until then he was tight on cash.

Massy pulled an envelope out of her jacket pocket. "Here's a bit to get you on your feet."

"Thanks." He hoped his unease didn't show on his face. This competent woman with ready cash and keys unsettled him a bit.

"The kitchen is stocked. Help yourself to anything. Get some rest. I'll come back later and we can discuss what you want to do for the resistance. Now that you're free to start a new life, think about what you really want to do with it."

"Sounds good." Questions hovered on Dirk's tongue but he didn't ask any of them. Massy's eyes were dark with secrets. He still didn't know what had triggered her running but he had a feeling she wasn't quite ready to tell him the truth.

Without another word, Massy left.

Dirk wandered through the apartment. He opened the refrigerator and pulled out a beer. He smiled at the label. Whoever had filled it either shared his tastes or was told by Massy his favorite brand. A bit of rifling through the drawers revealed a bottle opener. He popped off the lid and tossed it into the trash.

Glancing around, he groaned. "What am I going to do now?"

He'd thrown away his old life to help the resistance and get out from under the twins' rule. Time would tell if it was a good decision or not. For now he had no idea what to do with himself. Wallowing in self-pity appeared to be his plan of action. He settled on the couch and sucked down his beer.

A knock on the door pulled him out of his liquidy contemplation.

Curious over who would come see him, Dirk set down his bottle and headed for the door. He didn't bother checking who was on the other side. If they were bad guys, he couldn't exactly stop them from busting through.

Opening the door revealed Leon waiting…alone.

"Come in." Dirk stepped back to let Leon inside. "What can I do for you? Did you have some questions?"

Leon didn't answer until Dirk closed the door and automatically locked it behind him.

"I came to give you these." He handed over a thick packet.

Dirk popped the envelope open and peered inside. Tipping the container on its side released its contents. Travel and identification papers filled his palm, along with a thin cell phone. After walking farther into the apartment, he set everything on the table so he could go through it.

"These look good." They also were made in such a way that Dirk could go to whatever ward he wanted without being stopped. "These are all clean."

Leon smirked. "I only do the best."

"You did these yourself?"

When Massy had said Leon could get him papers, he'd figured the leader had someone on staff who dealt with that sort of stuff.

"Yep. When I joined the resistance, I had to start somewhere. Their forger had gotten too old to do the job. Without steady fingers he couldn't make them right. Instead, he showed me how to do everything. I passed on that knowledge to a few others, but I still make papers every once in a while so I don't lose my skill. You never know when it might come in handy."

"Huh." That made sense. "Well, they look great."

Leon couldn't stop staring at Dirk. It had been easy hiding his sexuality until now because there hadn't been anyone he'd been attracted to. That had all changed with Dirk. The blond's blue eyes twisted Leon in knots and made him want to do anything to remain Dirk's focus.

"I'm glad you approve."

Dirk flushed.

Leon stepped closer. He didn't think he was reading Dirk's expression wrong. Leon cupped Dirk's face.

"What are you doing?"

"Stop me if you don't want this." It would shatter him if Dirk turned away, but better to be warned now than to be punched later.

"Oh, I want." Dirk smiled. "I wasn't sure if you did."

Leon grabbed Dirk and yanked him closer. Before Dirk could say anything, Leon kissed him.

Yes!

Dirk's mouth slid across his in a press of heat and need. His cock lengthened. Instinctively, he rubbed against Dirk, pleased when a responding hardness pushed back at him. He wrapped his hands around Dirk's hips and held on tight.

A soft moan vibrated across his lips, raising his desire to levels he'd never experienced before. He'd held back the other times a man's gaze had warmed him. This time he couldn't. Some passions shouldn't be denied. If Dirk had turned him away, he would've marked it off as a lesson learned. Instead Dirk had responded...beautifully.

Their tongues tangled then retreated. Leon separated to gather more breath then dove in again. His fingers tightened, as if on their own accord, reluctant to release their prize.

"Have you ever had sex with a man before?" Leon had to know.

"Of course." Dirk frowned, as if not understanding the magnitude of Leon's question.

"I haven't," Leon confessed. "I-I've wanted to, but the right person never came along."

Dirk licked his lips. "Do you think I'm the right person?"

"If you aren't then the right one doesn't exist." His attraction to Dirk far surpassed the light sizzle of attraction he'd experienced before. This went beyond want and directly into need.

Dirk's mouth tilted up at one end. "I hope you're right. I'm definitely willing to try."

"Good." Leon didn't expect vows of forever but a nice 'let's give it a shot' was tons better than straight out rejection. "Let's take this to the bedroom."

"I'm hoping there is one." Dirk laughed. "I haven't explored the entire place."

Leon swept a gaze across the tiny room. "Didn't want the time commitment?"

Dirk shook with his amusement. "Something like that. Would you like a beer?"

"No. I want a bed." He refused to let their momentum die. If he gave Dirk time to think things over, Dirk might decide he could do better than a guy who hid from his needs and rarely gave into his desires.

A wicked grin crossed Dirk's face. "Well, I can't let it be said that I'm not a good host."

"No, that wouldn't be right," Leon agreed. He eagerly followed Dirk's fine ass as they walked down the hall.

Dirk opened a door then closed it. "Not that one."

His second choice must've been what he was looking for because he flashed Leon a bright smile then disappeared inside. Leon rushed to join him.

Inside were a double four-poster bed and a simple nightstand. A wardrobe took up one corner and a simple braid rug covered the wood floor.

"From what Massy said, this isn't what you're used to. Despite that, we're hoping you'll want to stay with us."

With me!

He had no reason to hope the younger man would remain just for him, but maybe he could use the lure of the resistance to keep him by Leon's side. They'd just met but Leon had been alone far too long and he hungered for companionship. As long as they were discreet, Leon knew the rest of the group would look the other way. Only if they flaunted their relationship would the others want to make an issue of it. He hoped Dirk didn't mind staying quiet. He wouldn't be a secret, exactly — they just wouldn't walk around holding hands.

"Strip." Dirk's hard command had Leon removing his clothes before his mind caught up with the order.

"Bossy," he scolded, even as he obeyed.

"Keep going," Dirk encouraged. He'd removed his suit jacket and tie. He'd stopped to watch Leon remove his shirt.

"Am I in this alone?"

"No. I just don't want to miss anything while I'm taking off my own clothes. You take yours off first then I'll take off mine."

Leon laughed. "I see." He couldn't find anything wrong with that plan. After quickly stripping, he climbed up on the bed and leaned his back against the headboard. "Go ahead. I'm ready."

Dirk's eyes widened as he examined Leon's naked form. "You're a fine man, Leon. I'm going to enjoy this."

"I'm glad you like what you see." Leon brutally fought back a blush. "I believe you owe me some clothing removal." He waved a hand, indicating Dirk's fully dressed state.

"Forgive me. I have been amiss," he said in a formal tone.

"Yes, you have."

With the same speed Leon had used, Dirk stripped naked.

Leon wiped his mouth to make sure he wasn't drooling. Although he'd fantasized about his first time with a man, he'd had no idea he'd be with someone as beautiful as Dirk. Not only was Dirk stunning, but he didn't act as if he knew it.

After he'd removed all his clothing, Dirk did a small spin so Leon could see him from all sides. "Good enough?"

"Oh, yes. More than." Leon crooked his finger at Dirk. He'd never been this lighthearted with a bed mate before. Of course, he'd only had women and they were always a bit uptight in his opinion. "No, come closer so I can do the full touching part. I believe this is a hands-on exhibit."

"It can be. It definitely can be." Dirk climbed up on the bed beside Leon.

Leon moaned over the silky slide of skin against skin.

"You feel amazing," Leon said.

"Same." Dirk kissed Leon and the sensations kept piling on.

Dirk's chest hair rubbed against Leon's, an intimate kiss of body to body. Leon sighed his appreciation. The hard rod pushing against him deserved attention. He wrapped his hand around Dirk's firm, hot length, gripping and pulling in alternating touches of gentle and rough until Dirk bucked into his hold, begging for more.

"I have so much more to give," Leon promised. "Whatever you want."

He bit his lip, almost wishing he could yank those words back. He had no idea where this might be going.

"You don't know me well enough to promise that." Dirk ran his fingers through Leon's hair—a drugging, soothing motion. "We will keep things simple this first time. If you feel adventurous later, just let me know." A wicked smile accompanied his words.

Leon didn't know how to respond to that. His cock didn't have the same problem. It hardened and rose alongside Dirk's, begging for attention. A hand, a finger—hell, just one more touch would push him over the edge.

Without warning, Dirk rolled them. Leon looked up into Dirk's amused blue eyes. "Something wrong?"

"Nope. You're right where I want you now."

Leon was used to being in charge. Since his parents' death at the hands of that bitch of a mob boss, he'd had to be on his own. Fifteen was a tough age to learn the facts of life, but he had hustled and got a job stocking shelves to keep food on his table and a roof over his head. For the first time since that fateful day, Leon was willing to let someone else hold sway over him.

Dirk slid his fingers across Leon's chest, an aimless pattern that had no goal other than to drive him out of his mind. Leon sucked in a breath and moaned beneath Dirk's touch.

"More!" Impatience clipped his words. He preferred a harder hold, a firmer grasp. Lifting his hips, he rubbed against Dirk's erection for two glorious movements until he spurted out his release in a messy display.

He blushed. "Sorry. I had hoped to last longer."

"It just means we need more practice."

Dirk's understanding smile soothed Leon's embarrassment.

Leon headed for the bathroom to clean up. The sound of footsteps had him looking over his shoulder.

"Let's take a shower." The wicked smile across Dirk's face had Leon's cock perking up.

A quick glance down confirmed what he'd suspected. "You didn't come."

"No. But I still have hope."

Leon's tension faded beneath Dirk's lighthearted teasing. This wasn't a man who'd bitch about Leon's performance or complain about his lack of experience. Dirk was a kind man who'd fallen in with a bad crowd. Leon knew as well as anyone the dangers of the mob bosses. Once they had their claws in a man, they didn't let him go.

"The water pressure isn't that great in this building," Leon warned.

"That's all right. As long as we can get wet."

There. Now his cock was ready again. "If you keep this up, I'll have a twenty-four hour erection around you."

They'd reached the bathroom and Leon turned to face his sexy new friend.

Dirk shook his head sadly. "I should take responsibility for my actions."

They waited until the shower heated, testing the water between kisses and touches. Hard muscle and smooth skin called to Leon with a siren's whisper.

"I can't get enough of you," he confessed.

"Good." Dirk stepped into the shower then stood beneath the stream, wetting his body.

Leon jealously watched the path of water droplets privileged enough to skim across Dirk's body. The liquid trail led to Dirk's hard cock. He licked his lips.

"Are you going to join me or just watch?" Dirk asked.

Leon blinked. "Sorry, I was just admiring the view." He had no other defense. He couldn't deny his staring. Luckily, Dirk didn't seem to mind.

"I prefer a more interactive experience." Dirk grinned. He reached out and pulled Leon closer.

If he didn't want to fall, Leon had to join Dirk. "Careful," he warned.

Dirk didn't release him. Rolling his eyes, Leon stepped beneath the spray. "Happy?"

"Oh, I am now." Dirk soaped up his hands then wrapped them around both of their erections.

"You could fuck me," Leon offered. Just the thought of Dirk pounding inside him had pre-cum dripping from his cock.

"I don't think you're ready for that."

"Maybe *you're* not ready for that," Leon said. As much as he appreciated Dirk's attention, he could tell Dirk wasn't quite ready to take things all the way.

"Maybe not, but we can still get off."

He continued pumping and squeezing their erections until, amid a chorus of gasps and groans, they spurted out their release, together. The water washed it away, leaving two wet and sated bodies in its wake.

Dirk released his grip on their cocks to cup Leon's face. His lips brushed in a soft slide against Leon's mouth. Leon sighed. What was it about this man that got to him? He'd denied himself for years but one glance at Dirk's blue eyes and he'd cast aside all his inhibitions to take a chance. "I *am* ready."

"Soon," Dirk agreed.

He'd take whatever he could of Dirk for as long as they lasted. He had no doubt they wouldn't stay together long. Soon Dirk would want to have a wife and kids of his own and cast aside his rebellious lover. Leon's devotion belonged to the people he was trying to save from oppression—not to one individual. But right this minute he belonged to Dirk, if only for a little while.

He kissed Dirk hard, pressing the shorter man against the shower wall. Leon had a few inches on Dirk, enough to make their kissing perfect. "I still want you to fuck me."

Dirk groaned. "If I screw you, you're going to be here all night."

Leon sighed. He couldn't spend the night. If anyone caught him leaving Dirk's apartment in the morning, still wearing the same clothes, questions would be asked that he wasn't quite ready to answer.

"I'm not ready to leave quite yet." He might have gotten off twice but he still didn't know much about Dirk.

"Then stay and have a beer. Surely you must sometimes visit to get to know newcomers."

"If I make you feel any more welcome, I might not survive." He didn't usually care if people were made comfortable. They either joined the resistance or didn't—Leon rarely swayed them one way or another.

Dirk smiled. Leon jolted at the quick kiss planted on his lips before Dirk moved away. He'd never been around anyone so affectionate before. He liked it. If only he could think of a way to overthrow the mobs and keep Dirk for himself.

They dressed quickly before desire took over their common sense. A knock on the door to Dirk's apartment confirmed the wisdom of their decision.

Dirk exchanged a look with Leon, who shrugged. "I'm not expecting anyone."

Opening the door revealed Massy on the other side.

"I couldn't find Leon to ask what he wants you to do." Without waiting for an invitation, she marched inside. "Oh." She stopped short when she saw Leon standing in the kitchen getting a beer. "There you are."

Leon froze. He hadn't expected to have to confront anyone yet. "Hey, Massy. I brought Dirk his papers."

And stayed for sex.

He doubted Massy missed the fact they both had wet hair from the shower. His explanation sounded hollow to his own ears. Massy didn't comment on it, but her smile looked forced as she glanced from one man to the next. "Oh…great. I guess I don't need to worry then. Is the information Dirk brought worthwhile?"

Leon nodded, more comfortable with this line of questioning. "I think it will really help. I've made a copy. I think we need to get it to someone in authority who might be able to take advantage of it. Just recycling it between resistance groups won't help. We need to unite."

"Who do you think?" Massy asked.

Leon ran his fingers through his damp hair then quickly retracted his hand. "Let me check with some contacts. I have a couple people in mind. We have to choose someone who is strong enough to stand up to the mob bosses and won't try to bury the information."

"Do you think they would?" Dirk asked.

"Of course, don't be naïve," Massy snapped. "They'd love to hide anything that makes them look bad."

"I hate to say it, but Massy is right." Leon's heart sank at Dirk's disappointed expression. "That doesn't mean we can't overcome this." He hated to disillusion anyone, especially someone new to the cause. The shiny glow of a fresh recruit faded quickly beneath reality.

"We're closer than ever to bringing them down," Massy said. Maybe she also sensed her brother's disappointment.

"Well, now you have your stuff. I'll talk to you both later." Leon awkwardly nodded to the siblings then took his leave.

Outside the apartment, he leaned against the wall and let out the breath he'd been holding. Damn, he'd never be able to hide his interest if this kept up. If they hadn't taken a break to shower, Massy might have caught them in the middle of things. He hoped Dirk had a better cover story to explain Leon's presence.

Chapter Three

Dirk met Massy's eyes without shame. He wouldn't apologize. He had nothing to be sorry for.

Massy opened her mouth then shut it again.

"What?"

"I don't know what to say. I didn't really think he'd go for you. I thought I was more his type."

Her disappointed expression twisted Dirk's conscience. She had told him of her interest in Leon, but he'd disregarded that in the heat of passion.

Dirk folded his arms. "Why didn't you think he'd go for me? You said yourself he was attracted."

"I wasn't certain he was gay."

"He might be bi." Dirk shrugged. He didn't care really, as long as Leon wanted him.

"Do you know why I joined the resistance?"

"Because the mobs are insane and ruining the city?"

"Well, yeah—that and because I met Leon at a resistance meeting. A friend of mine recommended that I go."

"Which friend?"

"Carly. Remember her? Her brother joined the resistance but was killed."

Dirk only vaguely recalled the news but nodded to get his sister to continue her tale.

"I thought he was gorgeous and so impassioned. I'd been thinking of a way to fight back against the mob. I hate the twins. Slimy bastards. Did you know the last time I went to see you at work, one of the twins grabbed my ass?"

"Which one?"

"Does it matter?"

"No, I guess not." Dirk gritted his teeth. He'd failed to protect his sister from the mob boss twins. He had no right to judge her. "What happened then?"

"I was so mad. I knew it wouldn't stop there." Her mouth took a grim set. Dirk wished he could argue and say the twins were harmless but he knew better. They took what they wanted and killed anyone who objected.

"So you went to a resistance meeting?"

Massy nodded. "Yeah. Carly said they were meeting that night. She was always trying to get me to join but I didn't because I knew if the twins found out, they'd hurt you. When I met Leon, I knew he could get me out of there."

"Why didn't you say anything to me?"

Massy sighed. "I thought the less you knew, the better off you'd be."

"You can see how that went." Dirk pointed at his face.

"Sorry."

"That's all right. Are you mad at me for fooling around with Leon?" He wouldn't insult her by pretending nothing happened.

"No. He's never wanted me. He helped me out when I needed it. The rest was me hoping for more."

"So we're okay?"

Massy nodded. "We're okay."

"Good." Dirk couldn't imagine what he'd do if Massy remained angry with him. Besides Leon, she was the only one he knew in the ward.

A loud siren pierced the air.

"What's that?" He clamped his hands over his ears.

"Come with me." Massy headed for the door. Dirk snatched up his papers and the cell phone. He didn't know where he'd end up but he wanted to be prepared.

In the short time since the alarm had begun, the hall had filled with people running. Dirk picked up his pace. He still didn't know what was going on, but the rush of people out of the building didn't seem like a drill. An air of anxiety and panic poured off the residents running and shoving.

"Is it a fire?" Dirk asked.

"Worse," a guy Dirk didn't recognize said. "Cops."

"Crap." Dirk couldn't risk getting a record. Even if he hadn't done anything wrong, if the authorities matched him with the resistance, they'd keep a close eye on him—something he couldn't afford in case his identification didn't hold up.

He lost sight of Massy in the cascade of people. Dirk panicked, frantically searching for any sign of her. While rushing down the stairs, he caught sight of Massy's dark head.

Racing after her, he ended up out on the street among the milling crowd. The people from the building quickly dispersed, probably each seeking a predetermined location. Someone grabbed his arm and jerked him out of the group.

Dirk almost fought back until he saw it was Leon.

"I lost Massy."

"She'll be fine. Let's go."

Dirk opened his mouth to argue but changed his mind. His sister had the instincts of a cat. If one of them were to be caught, it wouldn't be her.

Leon led Dirk to a diner with the words 'World's Best Pie' in the window.

"Is it?" Dirk pointed to the sign.

"I don't know if it's the world's best, but it's damn fine."

They entered the restaurant, quickly sitting where the waitress pointed. She wore thick-soled shoes and a formidable expression. Dirk wouldn't want to cross her.

The menus were tucked in a stand behind the salt and pepper. He snatched one up to examine his choices.

"The specials are blueberry pancakes and apple-raisin pie," the waitress announced, as she approached the table.

Dirk wrinkled his nose. He didn't like raisins or fruit in his pancakes. "I'll take a slice of your peach pie, please."

"Any coffee?"

"Yes. Black."

The waitress nodded then turned her attention to Leon. "The usual?"

"Yes, please."

She scribbled something on her pad then left.

Dirk watched the process with bemusement. "Come here often?"

"It's close to home and better than it looks."

"I hope so." Dirk held back from saying more. If Leon liked it there, he didn't want to offend his new lover.

Leon's eyes gleamed with amusement as if he could hear Dirk's thoughts.

"Here's your coffee." She set down a cup in front of Dirk and a glass of milk before Leon then walked away without another word.

"Don't like coffee?"

"Not with my food."

Dirk sipped his coffee and eyed Leon carefully. "You don't seem that upset."

"About what?"

"Having to vacate. You don't mind that you don't have a home to go to anymore?"

Leon shrugged. "That wasn't my home — that was a residence we were building. In a few weeks, a fake company will sell it and we'll use that cash to buy another one. We have them all around the city. When the alarm goes off, it triggers a lockdown of the basement. The cops won't find anything except a building of abandoned apartments. In a couple of days, people can go back and get their stuff. We'll find another building and start again."

"How can you live like that, moving over and over?"

"I do what I have to."

The sincerity in Leon's gaze had Dirk flinching. He'd never had that sort of commitment to anything before. He'd only come to the resistance to help out a friend. Although he wanted to bring down the mobs, he didn't know if he had that sort of willpower to forsake everything to the cause.

"Here's your pie." The waitress interrupted the moment by setting down the desserts in front of them.

"Thank you." A quick glance revealed Leon liked chocolate cream. "That looks good."

Leon smiled. "The best." He broke off a piece with his fork and held it up.

Dirk opened his mouth and let Leon feed him. It wasn't until he was chewing that he realized that probably wasn't the right thing to do with a man who wasn't out.

"That's good." He licked his lips, savoring the rich chocolate flavor.

Leon took a bite. "Yeah, it's one of the few that isn't too sugary. The baker uses dark chocolate."

Dirk ate a bite of his pie then dove in for more. "I'm willing to give them an award."

"They've already won several, even the ones the mob bosses fix."

They finished their pies without anything else said between them. Leon licked his lips when he finished. The coffee was terrible but the pie made up for it. He suspected it wasn't because he didn't like coffee with food that Leon had abstained from the bitter diner brew.

"What do we do now?"

"What do you mean?"

"Where do we go?" Dirk had enough money set aside to buy a new apartment every day but he didn't want this to be his life. He liked stability — one of the few reasons he'd stayed with the twins. Well, that and he couldn't leave.

"The residence team is setting up another apartment as we speak. They'll call me when it's ready."

Must be nice to have people. Dirk didn't say anything out loud. He couldn't afford to anger Leon — he needed as many allies as he could get.

Dirk's attention went to the television screen hung over the dining bar. "Looks like they arrested some of your people."

"*Our* people," Leon corrected.

Scenes from in front of the building showed police rounding up residents as they came outside. "What do you think they'll charge them with?"

Leon scowled. "Whatever they want."

Dirk continued to watch the screen. "Oh, hell."

He watched, helpless, as Massy was carted away by a burly policeman.

Leon's phone rang. He listened for a bit. "We're coming." He hung up. "Massy's been taken."

"I know." Dirk pointed at the screen. "What do we do now?"

"I need you to go down to the station, find out what the charges are and free as many of them as you can."

Dirk froze, the coffee cup halfway to his lips. He thought it over for a minute. He and Massy didn't look that much alike. She took after their dark-haired mother while he looked like their father. The police would have no reason to think they were related and look deeper into Massy's fake history.

"Okay, I can do that. Aren't you coming?"

Leon shook his head. "No, they know who I am. Go and bail her out. I doubt it will be much. They don't really have anything—they are just testing to see who will come for the people they arrested."

"Crap." Dirk didn't want to be under the eyes of the police. "If I give them my fake ID, they will have me under their notice."

Leon gripped Dirk's hand. "Be strong. You can't leave your sister behind bars."

"No. Of course not. She'd come for me." That was the truth. Massy would never leave him. He couldn't do that to her.

"Where's the police station?" Dirk wiped his mouth then tossed a few dollars on the table.

Leon pulled a small notebook and pen from his jacket pocket. He scrawled something down then handed it over. "Here you go. I put down my number too. Text me once you have Massy and I'll send you the address of the new place."

"All right." Dirk shoved it into his pocket.

He needed to go save his sister. He just hoped he didn't end up in jail.

Dirk left the restaurant without giving Leon the kiss he desperately wanted. Maybe one day he could kiss Leon whenever he chose but not now, when they were in the middle of a battle for control of their destinies. After spending his life under the thumb of the mobster twins, Dirk refused to let anyone push him around ever again.

The police station only took ten minutes to reach. As he walked up the steps, Massy was coming down them.

"Dirk!" She ran over and hugged him.

"Massy, what happened?"

"Our lawyer came and bailed us out. He threatened to make it public if they didn't let us go, since we hadn't done anything."

"And that worked?" Why hadn't Leon told him about a lawyer?

Massy grinned. "They might have the mobs, the judges and the cops on their side, but they don't have the ability to overpower everyone, at least not yet. We said there would be multiple strikes if they didn't let us go."

"Can you do that?"

"Yeah, the resistance is stronger here. We have some power. Not a lot, but some."

Dirk didn't understand the sly gleam in Massy's eyes but he went along with it. He pulled his phone out to text Leon about finding Massy.

"What are you doing?"

"Leon said to text him and he'd give me the location for the new building."

Massy snatched his phone. "You don't need to do that. I know the location."

"Hey, give that back."

A sharp pain in the back of his head sent him reeling to the ground. He blinked to focus his watering eyes when something struck him again and everything went black.

Chapter Four

Leon checked his phone for the tenth time. Where was Dirk? After not hearing from his lover for several hours, he decided to try Massy.

"Hello." Massy's voice sounded winded on the line.

"Massy, this is Leon. How are you doing?"

"Fine. I was released from jail. Did you need something?"

Leon scowled. A sense of unease slithered through him. "Have you seen your brother? I need to send him our new address."

"Oh, no. I haven't seen him recently. Not since evacuation. Why don't you just send them to me and if I see him, I'll pass it along."

"Sure. I'll text them to you." Leon quickly hung up.

How did she get out?

"Jimmy, did any of the others get released yet?"

The first person Leon had contacted after having pie with Dirk was his right hand man. Jimmy had gone through several evacuations with him and he had yet to let Leon down. His friend's ability to coordinate large moves made him an invaluable aide.

Jimmy typed into his phone for several minutes before pressing 'Send'.

They both waited until a soft ping indicated Jimmy had a message. "No. No one's been released."

"Massy has. I just talked to her on the phone. She says she hasn't seen her brother."

Jimmy frowned. "You know what that means."

Leon sighed. "We have another traitor."

"On the plus side, we've only had five in all the years we've been doing this," Jimmy said.

"Yeah, I guess that's something." A lot of wards had constant betrayal. Somehow the fact Massy had turned on her own brother was one of the worst. "At least she doesn't have the information."

"No, but her brother might know what it is," Jimmy warned.

"I doubt it. He was just a messenger. He said he didn't know anything when he gave it to us, and I believe him."

"The question is, how much did Massy tell the Widow? Does she know how close you two are?"

Leon had immediately confided to Jimmy his encounter with Dirk. He'd had to share with someone and Jimmy already knew he was gay.

"Oh, fuck." Leon clenched his fists. Massy knew exactly how close he was to her brother. "I wonder if that's why she did it. She's always had a little crush on me. Arrange a street team to pick her up. If nothing else, maybe we can find out how much she tattled."

"Will do." Jimmy didn't make any comment. His fingers flew over his phone as he put out the word.

Leon groaned. Trust him to be attracted to the one guy who could destroy him.

* * * *

Massy glared at Leon from her position tied to a chair. "I don't know why you are trying to pin this on me. How do I know where my brother went?"

"That's the question. Why is it that you are the only one released? I've asked around and no one else had a lawyer come for them."

"Maybe I'm lucky." Massy's scornful glance revealed to Leon that she didn't care one way or another if he believed her story.

"Or maybe you're a lying bitch who needs me to knife you." Jimmy flashed out his dagger and pressed it to the top of Massy's cheek.

For the first time, her smug expression slipped. "You can't do that. I'm innocent." She began to tremble beneath Jimmy's blade.

"Innocent people don't lie. We got surveillance of you talking to your brother then stepping aside while he hit the pavement. Who was the man who punched him?" It had taken them hours, but they had a bit of surveillance camera footage that showed a large guy smashing Dirk in the back of the head with a brick.

"S-she promised to give me a position in her organization," Massy blurted out.

Jimmy removed the knife. "You sold your own brother for a job. Wow, and people say I'm cold."

"You don't know how hard it is to be a woman in a mob-infested city. This could be my one chance to get respect." Massy sneered. "My stupid brother always has to stand in my way."

"I'm sorry, but I'm out of tiny violins," Leon snapped. "Now where's Dirk?"

Massy shrugged. "I don't know. She didn't tell me. I just had to give him to her."

"And you didn't care what happened to him afterward?" Leon finished. "You should be happy I don't hit women, because if you'd been Dirk's brother instead of sister, I would've killed you for the pure joy of it. Some types of evil don't deserve to breathe the same air. Take her to a holding cell."

"Wait! What are you going to do with me?" Massy shouted.

"I don't know yet. A lot will depend on whether Dirk comes back alive or not."

He could hear Massy's screams echoing down the tunnel as Jimmy dragged her off. He ran a hand through his hair. Poor Dirk. What could he possibly be going through?

* * * *

"Would you like some more tea?" The White Widow held up a small teapot.

"No, thank you. It's been delicious." Dirk ate another crisp cookie and sipped his tea. Despite the throbbing in his head, the White Widow was an excellent hostess.

"It's not often I get to keep company with such a lovely young man. Most men try to grope me within minutes of meeting." She set down the teapot and smoothed her skirt.

Dirk swept an eye across her carefully coiffed hair, high cheekbones and perfect makeup. If he were inclined toward the female persuasion, he might be tempted, if it weren't for the cold calculating look in her eyes. "I try to be a gentleman," he replied.

The Widow laughed. "I think it's more that you *prefer* gentlemen."

Dirk set down his cup, his stomach churning with tension and cucumber sandwiches. "Why would you say that?"

"Oh, relax. I'm not judging. I don't care who you love. In this case, it will be to my benefit. I bribed your sister but I lied about hiring her. If she will turn on her own brother, what would she be willing to do to me? I expect loyalty in those I hire. I doubt she understands the word."

He hated just a little that he completely agreed with the vile woman across from him. "What do you want with me?" He didn't want to discuss his sister. The bite of betrayal was still a fresh wound.

The Widow seemed to think about it, as she stirred her tea with a tiny spoon. "I want you to tell me what kind of information you brought to the resistance."

"I don't know what it was."

Her red lips, the only stripe of color on her face, thinned into a fine line. "I can have you killed!"

"That won't change the fact that I don't know what is in the information I brought."

"Then get it for me!" she growled. "I'll let you go if you promise to bring me the information."

"You'd trust me?" He doubted she'd risen to her current level by trusting anyone.

The Widow laughed, a high, grating sound that scraped against Dirk's eardrums. "Of course not. I'd have you tagged. I can't risk you disappearing into the muck of the resistance. Instead you can be my spy. Get the information and I will free you."

"And if I don't?"

She smiled, revealing a set of perfect teeth. "I'll have you killed." She said the words with the same tone as someone commenting on the beauty of the weather.

Dirk's mouth dried up as fear slammed into him. He knew she would kill him if given the chance. And if he did find the information, she'd kill him anyway. "All right. I'll do it."

"Excellent. My man on the inside can get you what I need. I would've had him bring it to me, but I've worked hard to keep no connection between us. It's hard to place good spies."

A sick, churning, twisting in his stomach had him swallowing a few times before he blurted out the question. "Who?"

She tapped the spoon to the brim of her teacup. "Jimmy. Do you know him?"

"Yeah, I do." Rage built in him and Dirk wished he could throttle Jimmy with his bare hands.

First his sister, then Leon's right hand man. There were apparently few loyal people in the world, and with his promised betrayal, Dirk couldn't exactly throw any stones.

So caught up on watching the Widow, he didn't hear anyone coming up behind him until there was a pinch in back of his neck.

Dirk gasped.

"We wouldn't want you to start thinking you got away with anything. The tracker we injected will let us know your every move."

Her cold smile of triumph burned a hot fire in his chest. He'd get even if it was the last thing he did.

"I don't know where they are going to be. Massy took my phone."

"Here." A male voice said behind him. His phone was handed over his shoulder.

He didn't dare look behind him. The less he knew, the smaller the chances were they going to kill him.

"Thank you." He slipped the phone into his jacket pocket, eager to get out of there. He needed to see Leon. Once he talked to him, he would decide what to do next. A tracker in his neck only told them where he was, not what he was doing.

"Now get going. We have plans to make." The Widow waved a hand at him as if shooing off a particularly nasty insect.

He planned to be much more damaging than that.

He stood and headed for the door, not bothering to glance at anyone else in the room. They were of no importance. He had a man to meet.

As soon as his shoes hit the sidewalk, he pulled his phone back out to text Leon. He paused for a moment before just sending a note that said *Free*.

A few seconds later his phone beeped with an address on its screen.

"Good."

At least now he knew where to go. He hoped Massy hadn't beaten him there.

The address turned out to be only a few blocks away from the White Widow. A condemned sign hung drunkenly to one side. After taking a quick glance around to make sure he wasn't followed, Dirk ducked beneath the tape and pushed open the door.

The metal rectangle swung inward without a squeak.

Definitely the right place.

Noises came from the end of the hall. Dirk followed them to an open apartment. Leon, Jimmy and several people he'd never had the opportunity to meet were converged around a computer.

"Leon."

"Dirk! You made it!"

He glanced at the suspicious faces around Leon. "Can I talk to you for a moment?"

"Sure." Leon didn't ask why he needed to speak to him alone—he simply stood up and headed his way.

Dirk grabbed Leon's wrist and pulled him further along the hall. "Massy turned me over to the White Widow."

"I know. She told us."

"She's here?" Dirk glanced up and down the hall.

"She's being held in a restraining cell until we can decide what to do with her. I don't take betrayal lightly." Leon narrowed his gaze. "What did you have to agree to in order to get free?"

Leon bit his lip. "They injected me with a tracking device. She says she will detonate it if I don't bring her the information I brought you."

"Where?"

"Where what?"

"Where's the tracking device?"

"In the back of my neck."

"We need to get it out!"

"Is there a problem?" Jimmy popped his head out of the apartment.

Dirk flashed Jimmy a cool look. "She also said Jimmy was a plant of hers."

"You aren't going to believe him, are you?" Jimmy's voice pierced the hall in a loud shriek.

Leon spun around. "Is this true?"

"Of course not. I've been with you forever." Jimmy glared at Leon. "You're the one suspiciously free."

"I told Leon what I had to do to get free. What did you do?"

He knew he'd found the truth when Jimmy paled.

"Wh-what do you mean?"

"Jimmy..." Leon's soft, heart-broken voice froze Jimmy's protest on his lips.

"She was going to kill my parents, Leon. I had to agree."

Leon backed away from Jimmy to stand by Dirk's side. "Why didn't you tell me?"

"Because unlike him, I have something to lose. I don't want my parents dead. He doesn't fucking have anyone so he can be all selfish and do what he wants." Jimmy glared at Dirk. "Bastard."

Dirk gripped Jimmy by the shirtfront and slammed him into the wall. "You don't get to be self-righteous. I'm sorry about your parents, but if we bring down the mob then the White Widow isn't going to be around to threaten anyone."

"Let's get that tracker off you. Then we can go to Plan C."

Dirk looked over his shoulder at Leon. "What's Plan C?"

"Completely underground. We've dug a tunnel to Ward Two—now's the time to open it up. We need to get to Cesar and let him know we've been successful. With our encryption program, we've been able to send the information to the rest of the wards. Unfortunately Ward Two doesn't have a good tech person. He has to hear the news from someone he trusts."

"So I risked my life for nothing?" Anger poured through him.

Leon gripped Dirk's arms. "No. You didn't. We're the only group that could disseminate the information to everyone else. Cesar needs to know he's now free to act. Without knowing if everyone got the intel, he couldn't move forward."

"Who are you going to send?"

Leon's expression had Dirk shaking his head.

"Yes. I have to be the one," Leon insisted.

"Not without me, you don't. I'm not letting you take on something like this without me." Dirk had risked too much to let Leon throw everything away.

Leon gazed into Dirk's eyes after a moment he nodded. "All right."

"You're just going to trust him? It took me years—*years* before you trusted me!" Jimmy shouted.

Leon pinned Jimmy with a cold look. "And now I know I should've gone with my first instincts and kept you out. Help me get the bug out of Leon."

Jimmy folded his arms across his chest. "Why should I?"

"Because if you don't, I'll shoot you for the traitor you are." Leon pulled a gun from beneath his jacket and pointed it at Jimmy.

Jimmy paled. "Got it. Bring him in here and I'll get the first aid kit."

"Make a wrong move, Jimmy, and I will end you."

He hadn't heard that tone from Leon before and Dirk hoped it was never directed toward him.

The little piece of metal took a great deal of effort and a lot of pain to remove. They had a first aid kit but no anesthesia. Dirk suspected Jimmy enjoyed cutting the tracker out of his skin.

Jimmy slapped a bandage on the back of Dirk's neck. "All fixed."

"Hurt him again and I'll shoot out your kneecaps," Leon growled.

Jimmy swallowed audibly. "Yes, sir."

"Everyone vacate!" Leon shouted.

"What are you going to do with Massy?" Dirk asked. After everything she'd done, she was still his sister.

Leon grinned. "Don't worry—I have a plan." He handed the beacon over to Jimmy. "You know what to do with this."

* * * *

"Let me out of here!" Massy shook the metal bars, screaming.

Loud footsteps sounded in the corridor.

"Thank fuck. Finally! You going to give me something to…eat—?" She backed away from the door when she saw who was visiting. "What are you doing here?"

"We've come to rescue you. You should be grateful." The White Widow stepped close to the bars. "I've decided I might have a use for you after all. I could use some more couriers for the less savory parts of town."

Massy paled. "But they'll kill me."

The Widow smiled. "If you're lucky."

Massy closed her eyes. She hoped Leon got the information where it needed to go soon. Otherwise she might not survive her new employment.

* * * *

"Ready for this?" Leon asked.

They stood before the solid security door leading to the secret tunnels. The numbers glowed, beckoning Leon to enter the right code.

Dirk nodded, his mouth set in a firm line. "Yeah, let's go."

Leon punched a complicated series of numbers. "It's just you and me now, Dirk. Time to save the world."

"Well, at least our little piece of it," Dirk conceded.

"Yeah, our little piece." Leon slid his hand in Dirk's, entwining their fingers. He didn't know what the future held for them, but he was ready to explore it and see. He refused to live in fear either from bigots or mobsters or corrupt police. The time to stop them was now.

The steel door swung open to the combined scents of stale air and rich earth. Light filtered through the tunnel from a series of small holes. Dirk took a deep breath beside him.

"Let's go."

Together, the two men went through then closed the door behind them. They had a man to find and a mission to finish before they could concentrate on the most important thing...each other.

BONFIRE HEART

Devon Rhodes

Dedication

For the other four ladies in this anth — thanks for
taking a different turn this year.
And for Carol — we missed you! Thank you for all you
do, busy lady.

Chapter One

Thierry Alexander grimaced inwardly as he rounded the corner and saw the mayor coming straight toward him, though he had enough presence of mind—and practice in concealing his true emotions—to keep his facial expression from giving him away.

"Alexander, good. I'm glad I caught you before you left." The salt and pepper hair was perfectly sprayed into place as always, and the mayor was dressed for success in an expensive suit. From his outer appearance, he was the picture of benign political authority. But Thierry knew he was anything but the benevolent, people-oriented leader that the media was coached to portray.

"Mayor," he greeted. He sensed Eduardo, who had been walking at his side with his rolling garment bag on the way downstairs to the car, stepping away unasked to give them privacy. That was to be expected. The mayor made no secret of his disdain for Thierry's assistant, and would likely have ordered Eduardo to leave them.

"Walk with me." The mayor didn't wait for a response but led the way slowly down the hall.

People gave them a wide berth as they proceeded.

"All set for your trip to New York and Boston?"

"Yes. Just heading down to the car now to catch my flight," Thierry hinted.

"It'll wait for you." Apparently the mayor wasn't always as oblivious as Thierry had hoped. "I'm guessing that our Immigration Bill will be a topic of conversation after hours," the mayor got straight to the main point of the conversation.

Thierry gave a brief nod. "That's to be expected. It's a big move for Chicago." Which was a major understatement.

The Bill was being touted as a step forward, allowing more freedom of movement for classes of people who'd traditionally had a hard time affording the travel papers, or who had been disqualified from moving around the city — or out of it — for one reason or another. However, Thierry and Eduardo had heard whispers behind the scenes about it having a more nefarious purpose. No leopard changed its spots that quickly...unless it was deliberately camouflaging itself. The political system in Chicago was beyond corrupt — it was dangerous. And the United States had very little say in what happened in the city. It would take almost an act of war to get the US to intervene in state affairs.

"I trust you'll be a good ambassador as usual, particularly for the Bill and its benefit to the people of Chicago."

"Of course," Thierry automatically agreed. That was his job, after all — being a genuinely good public face on the rotten body of Chicago's governance.

It turned his stomach.

He could feel his legendary patience slipping. A hint of movement to his right—Eduardo was evidently anxious to get him away from the mayor as well. Whether it was because he didn't want Thierry to run late or because he sensed his impatience was a toss-up.

"My apologies, Mayor, but Deputy Mayor Alexander needs to—"

"Fine, fine." The mayor gave Eduardo a slight sneer that put Thierry's back up.

He swallowed down his distaste, transferred his briefcase to the other hand and held out a hand to shake. "Thank you for your time, sir." He hated having to toady to the slimeball, but the only way to stay in a position to possibly do anything about the city's blight was to play along. It was a dance of mutual need and distrust between Thierry and his few allies, like Eduardo, and the rest of the damn power players in the city.

With one last hard grip, the mayor let go of Thierry's hand. He barely kept from wiping it on his pants, then tipped his head in a goodbye before striding down the hall, Eduardo at his side.

Once they'd reached the elevator, Thierry chanced a look at Eduardo, who appeared supremely irritated. It made him smile.

"Really? What on earth can you find funny about getting stopped by that...*pendejo*," Eduardo finished in silence by mouthing the insult in Spanish.

"Nothing really. Just glad to be heading out. I've been looking forward to this trip." All except for the fact that he'd be missing Eduardo. "Are you sure you can't come with?"

"I wish." The glance that Eduardo shot Thierry then was more than that of an assistant wanting to travel with his boss—it was definitely that of a lover.

Thierry cleared his throat. Last thing he needed was to walk out of the elevator with an erection. When the doors opened, they headed toward the back hallway together.

"I'll need you to ride to the airport with me," Thierry decided.

Eduardo gave him side-eye, but played along for whatever audience they might have. "Good idea, sir. It was a very busy morning. I never got a chance to go over the latest reports with you."

They had been busy, all right, but no—they hadn't done much work.

Thierry led the way out past security to the below-ground loading dock where the bulletproof limo was waiting. Eduardo handed the suitcase to the chauffeur then got in through the open back door of the car. Thierry followed him inside, keeping his briefcase with him, and settled onto the seat at a respectable distance from Eduardo.

"Sir?" The chauffeur—who, like all their drivers, doubled as a bodyguard—bent down to look in through the door from Thierry to Eduardo and back, obviously wondering about the deviation from the plan.

"My assistant and I need to do some work on the way to the airport. After you drop me at the jet, please bring him back here," Thierry instructed. He vaguely recognized the driver, but wasn't sure as to the man's affiliation, whether to the mayor, to the resistance or to one of the gang families. He'd find a way of asking Eduardo after they were underway. It was always hard to know whom to trust.

"Yes, sir." The driver closed the door then walked around to get into the driver's seat. Without being asked, he raised the privacy glass.

Eduardo smirked at him and lifted an inquiring eyebrow as the car began slowly moving.

There was still an excellent chance that the driver or someone else was listening in, but as long as they watched what they said, what they chose to do away from prying eyes could be put down to simply getting off.

And Eduardo knew that as well as Thierry did.

"Sir? Pardon my saying so, but you look a little...tense. Is there anything I can do to help relax you before your trip?"

Thierry grinned at the devilish look on Eduardo's face as he played his part of 'assistant' perfectly... Well, if they were starring in a low-budget porno. "Hmm. I suppose it has been a stressful morning, and it'll be a long day traveling..." They'd had sex last night then rubbed off together in the shower this morning, but anticipation had his cock thickening in his suit pants.

Eduardo moved suddenly to his knees on the floor between his legs and he parted his thighs even farther to accommodate him.

"Oh, sir, you're very stiff here." He cupped Thierry's firming cock. "That can't be comfortable."

"These pants are pretty confining. Open them up and take me out." Thierry gave Eduardo a fond smile that belied his gruff order.

"Yes, sir." Eduardo unzipped his pants.

Thierry shifted in his seat as Eduardo quickly fished inside his open fly and boxers and took him in hand. He was completely hard by the time the heated skin of his shaft was exposed to the cool air. Eduardo looked up at him and winked before engulfing the head in the perfect heat of his mouth.

He slid his mouth down his cock and Thierry's eyes drifted closed for a few moments. God, his lover's mouth was incredible, and the years they'd been together ensured that Eduardo knew him intimately. From the light strokes along the insides of his thighs to the gentle pressure under his balls, Eduardo played to every one of his hotspots as he sucked him toward completion.

Who knew whether they were actually being monitored at the moment, but Thierry restrained himself from talking or making any noise. That seemed too intimate a thing to express while they were actually sharing pleasure, even though they had started off playing their parts.

So he contented himself with running his hand over Eduardo's silky, dark hair, and caressing his cheek with his thumb. His climax started in his balls with an intense tingling that peaked almost too fast to warn Eduardo. He tried giving his shoulder a tug, but Eduardo refused to move and relaxed his suction enough so Thierry could thrust unimpeded into the surrounding warmth as he came.

"Come here," he whispered.

Eduardo gave one last suck then a kiss on the tip before sitting back on his heels. His lips were puffy and red—and Thierry was convinced anew that he was the sexiest man Thierry had ever seen.

Thierry let his gaze drift suggestively down to Eduardo's fly, but he shook his head before leaning forward to kiss Thierry.

"Why not? I'm sure we have time," he murmured against Eduardo's lips.

"Hold that thought until you get home." Eduardo gave him one last kiss then resumed his place on the seat. Thierry fixed his clothing then noticed Eduardo removing his cell phone from his pants pocket. Not his usual one, but his other one.

The one he used as Cesar, the head of Chicago's resistance movement.

Eduardo entered a passcode then swiped a couple of times before frowning at the screen. He wore an expression Thierry was very familiar with—intense concentration as his brain clicked along.

Thierry rested his hand on Eduardo's thigh to get his attention.

In response, Eduardo held up his phone, showing a text from a number Thierry wasn't familiar with.

COD package held for your pick-up. Signature and proof of ID required.

Thierry shrugged to indicate that he didn't understand. It was innocuous, but the fact that it had come in on his lover's 'Cesar' phone meant it was probably some kind of code.

Thierry would have to wait to get back from his trip before he could freely talk to Eduardo about this, but he tried to get some sense of what it was about. "Good?" he asked, referring to the text, but trying to keep it audibly relevant to their previous actions.

"The best," Eduardo replied, and his expression altered slightly. It was no less intense but underlying that was a hint of...hope?

Chapter Two

Eduardo paced his small bedroom impatiently as he waited for the text he hoped to receive asap. He and all of the other house staff knew that Thierry was back in residence tonight. His position as deputy mayor meant that he was one of the few in Chicago who regularly traveled freely around and out of the city. Since the mayor didn't like to leave his domain for fear that one of the stronger gang leaders would take advantage of his absence, Thierry was the de facto ambassador for the city. His natural charisma and intelligence made him perfect for that job…and his ability to act didn't hurt either.

While Eduardo always worried about Thierry when he was gone, he was more anxious to reunite with him than ever. The information he'd finally received yesterday was momentous—life-changing, and not just for the two of them. It was what they'd been waiting for and working toward for such a long time…

His phone buzzed on the tabletop, and he snatched it up.

My suite asap.

Eduardo had to smile. So terse, but it had to be. They were very careful to not give any hint of an emotional connection between them, and texts were, after all, a written record. In this day and age, it was the height of stupidity to put anything in writing—especially electronic—that you wouldn't want your enemies to discover. The more innocent of the household and their watchers probably didn't think anything of his role as Thierry's personal assistant. Cynical sorts likely thought Thierry used him for sexual satisfaction.

Which was true, but in the privacy of darkness they had much more than that.

He strode down the hall, carefully avoiding looking at anyone he passed, and there were several people around. Most of the staff were spies for one faction or another—either the mayor or occasionally one of his enemies. Not much they could do about that, but at least they had found a way to keep Thierry's bedroom from close scrutiny. He'd set up his private work desk in there rather than in the outer room of his suite, citing concerns that someone he might meet with there could see information or documents that weren't for public knowledge. So, for the same reason, his bedroom had become exempt from surveillance.

As he approached the suite, he noticed with relief that Matt was on guard duty. He was one of the nicer bodyguards assigned to Thierry. At least he didn't sneer at Eduardo or hassle him like a few of the others.

"Hola, Eduardo." The pronunciation of Matt's greeting was appalling but it tickled Eduardo that he even tried. Actually, it was a bit of a risk. 'Cultural

deviation' it was termed, and in some wards it was against the law. Not as a primary offense, but something they could tack on if you were detained or arrested for something else. That was fairly new and part of an alarming trend of late.

"*Hola*, Matt." Time to nip that in the bud. "Careful about that," he murmured as he got closer. "He sent for me," he said in a normal tone of voice, not waiting for a response to his soft rebuke.

"Right." Matt still removed his phone from his pocket and followed the protocol of calling Thierry to confirm, as he did every time. "Mr Alexander? Eduardo Chavez Morales is here." He paused to listen. "Yes, sir." He hung up and nodded to the key pad. "Go ahead."

It was both reassuring and a bit daunting that the guard who knew them so well and was the most sympathetic still went to such lengths to follow the rules to 'protect' Thierry.

Eduardo entered the passcode and waited for the green light and the click before opening the door to the suite. "I may be a while," he told Matt, who didn't bat an eye.

"I'll be here until his usual breakfast time."

That was good to know. He'd make sure to leave before Matt went off duty. The next guard might not be so pleasant about Eduardo leaving in the morning after 'working all night'.

Once he'd closed the door behind him and heard the electronic lock engage, he went through his usual routine of straightening the outer room, doing his job while simultaneously looking for anything unusual or out of place. He was dying to see Thierry by this point, but the last thing he wanted, especially now, was to deviate from the norm.

It looked like Thierry had just sloppily dumped everything in the living room in his impatience to get comfortable once he was home, but Eduardo knew that whenever items had been out of his immediate control, he didn't want them in the bedroom in case they'd been bugged. So he hung up the jackets, opened the suitcase and emptied it, sorting the contents into laundry and dry cleaning bags in the hall closet then put his umbrella in the stand by the door. He'd take a closer look at everything in the morning. His briefcase was nowhere to be seen, so Thierry must be confident that no one had tampered with it and had taken it into the bedroom.

Once he was done, he crossed to the bedroom door and rapped lightly. "Mr Alexander?"

The door was yanked open almost before he stopped knocking. "About time, Eduardo. When I tell you I need you, I mean immediately." The scold was delivered mostly for whatever audience might be listening, but Eduardo also read the very real impatience and want in Thierry's eyes.

"Sorry, sir." He tried to keep the smile from his lips.

"Well, come in then." Thierry walked into the bedroom, leaving Eduardo to follow him.

Eduardo closed the door and locked it, then turned around just in time to brace himself. Thierry thumped him up against the wall.

"God, that trip felt like it took forever. Why didn't you come with me again?" Thierry didn't wait for an answer to his murmured question but took Eduardo's mouth in a ravishing kiss that demanded his participation.

Thierry might be the hope on which the city's resistance had their future pinned, but right now he was just a man, and Eduardo knew that he'd be in more of a mood to listen after he'd assuaged his need to reconnect, a need he fully shared. He slid his arms around Thierry's waist and pulled him snug against him, opening to his kiss. The onslaught gentled with his compliance and Eduardo slowly took control, petting Thierry's mussed hair back from his temple before cupping his jaw. Thierry groaned into his mouth and rotated his groin, wordlessly pleading.

Eduardo swiftly changed their positions until he had Thierry pressed back against the wall, grinding his hard cock along the matching erection under Thierry's suit pants.

He broke off the kiss and ran his lips lightly along the stubble of Thierry's cheek until he reached the smooth hollow below his ear. Thierry arched his head, baring his neck, but Eduardo didn't dare to mark him, so he gave a small nip then ran his teeth along his jaw line before returning to his mouth.

"Cesar…"

"Shh."

Thierry's need and probable exhaustion was now clear—otherwise he never would have slipped and called Eduardo by his nickname, even in the privacy of his bedroom. He scrutinized Thierry's drawn face and the redness to his eyes, finally seeing the signs.

That put a slightly different spin on the night. He pulled away and tugged Thierry after him toward the bed. "Come on." He began to unbutton the top couple of fastenings of his shirt, just enough to be able to pull it off over his head. As soon as his hands were clear, Thierry began to try to undo Eduardo's pants.

"Do your own," he ordered, gently redirecting them to Thierry's pants. As soon as he had undone his tie and had begun to unbutton his shirt, Thierry relaxed a bit and started to strip.

"Good idea. Sorry. I'm just—"

"It's okay. I know."

"You don't," Thierry argued, kicking his pants aside. Eduardo forced himself to not go pick them up as Thierry continued, "It's more than that."

"I had a feeling. We can talk after," he soothed, finishing his own striptease. He followed Thierry up onto the bed, admiring the pale expanse of skin that rarely saw the sun. Thierry was several inches taller than him, but almost fragile-looking in his thinness. He seldom had time to eat a full meal, and Eduardo would wager that he hadn't eaten at all this evening. He often forgot to eat, and the lifestyle and scrutiny he lived under didn't help.

As much as he loved to look at Thierry's naked form, Eduardo knew that his lover felt the chill much more easily than he, so he forced Thierry to move so he could pull back the covers then urged him under them. Joining him, he wrapped himself around Thierry, who gave a satisfied sigh.

"You just want to warm up and sleep? Or you want this?" He set up a rubbing motion that sent his cock sliding against Thierry's belly and his shaft.

Thierry reached down and Eduardo's head went back at the firm grasp on his erection. "I want you to fuck me. That'll warm me up just fine. Then we can sleep for a bit, but..."

They did have a lot to talk about. "Don't worry. I'll be sure to wake you up after a short" —*or long*—"nap." His hand wasn't idle while he reassured Thierry, who arched into his touch as he glided his fingers along his flank, his cock, his abdomen in random, teasing patterns.

Thierry made a noise of frustration in his throat and grabbed his hand, pressing it harder against him.

Eduardo grinned and reached back to fumble in the magazine pocket of the antique side table for the lube. He had to let go and sit up briefly to accomplish the task, but finally was able to slick up his fingers.

Thierry bent his upper leg in anticipation, knowing by now that Eduardo loved to prepare Thierry while spooning him. He rewarded him with kisses down the cord of his neck to his shoulder as he gently entered Thierry with his fingers.

He took his time and soon had Thierry gasping and squirming with need. Eduardo's cock hardened even further at the audible evidence of his lover's readiness, and after one more application of lube, to both Thierry's hole and his shaft, he gave them both what they wanted and pressed the head of his cock into the valley of his ass cheeks.

After notching into place, he wrapped his arms tightly around Thierry. It only took a practiced flex of his hips before he sank the head into the warm grasp of Thierry's ass.

"Oh, yes." Thierry held onto Eduardo's embrace as if refusing to allow him to ever let go, and he pressed back, taking more of his cock in.

"Thi," he breathed against his ear. "I missed you." He set up a firm rhythm intended to speed up the process rather than draw things out and took Thierry's erection in hand.

Thierry wasn't arguing in the least, meeting his thrusts with little tips of his pelvis. "Missed you. I hate being apart. Hate sleeping alone."

"Yeah." They couldn't be sure of their surroundings while traveling, though, so even if he'd accompanied him as his assistant, they couldn't have slept together. And they couldn't afford a scandal. Thierry's squeaky clean image was why he was in the position he was in.

Even the criminal factions running the city recognized the need for a poster child who was above reproach. Thierry struggled with appearing as a cover for their activities but the truth was, it allowed him to work behind the scenes to try to effect change. It was a trade-off that he handled better on some days than others.

Eduardo increased the speed and pressure of his hand, though he kept his hips at the same steady pace, and soon Thierry turned his face to kiss then bite Eduardo's biceps. His channel tightened just before he came in Eduardo's hand, and the increased pressure soon had Eduardo faltering in his rhythm then holding tight against Thierry.

"Ahhh, *querido*," he sighed as he came.

Thierry ran his hand back over Eduardo's hip to hold him in place, which Eduardo allowed for a couple of minutes. Soon, he had no choice but to disengage himself against the sleepy murmurs of protest.

Eduardo rose, cleaned up then kissed Thierry as he passed him on the way into the bathroom to take his turn. After walking around to the opposite side of the bed, he climbed in then held the covers up for Thierry as he quickly returned to join him.

Linking their fingers against the mattress then stroking Thierry's upper arm with the other hand, Eduardo tried to clear his mind and simply enjoy his lover's presence in his arms. But he knew sleep would be a long time coming for him. Lots to discuss, but no words were necessary just then as Thierry settled in for some much needed rest.

The crazy world out there could wait a bit longer.

Chapter Three

"Thi. Wake up."

Thierry inhaled sharply as his eyes popped open. Disoriented, not sure for a moment where he was, he sat straight up, trying to focus. God, he was too exhausted to think.

"Hey, I gotcha. It's just me. You're home."

Warm, familiar arms and an equally familiar lightly accented voice soothed him, and his eyes drifted closed as he leaned to his right against a strong chest.

"Now, don't you go back to sleep on me. Hmm?"

"'M not," he managed to croak. How long had he been asleep? Felt like about ten minutes.

"You got about six hours, but we have a little bit of work to do, then I have to leave before the breakfast changeover. Why don't you go shower and try to wake up? I'll brew some coffee."

That was a damn fast six hours. Thierry felt like he needed about six more. He opened his eyes to look into Eduardo's warm brown ones. After a brief, tender kiss, he stood up and stretched, noting that Eduardo had evidently already showered and was dressed. His dark hair was still a bit damp and he smelled like Thierry's soap.

It was a good scent on him.

His cock stirred and he absently rubbed it.

"Stop that or we'll never get anything done."

"Sheesh. Okay, fine. I'm going."

Eduardo patted his ass as he walked by, and that simple touch soothed more than aroused, thankfully. He took a quick shower and brushed his teeth. When he emerged from the bathroom, the scent of coffee greeted him.

"Get dressed first." Eduardo was sitting at his desk focused on the computer. Two steaming mugs were sitting on the small café table between the wing chairs near the window. He glanced up and, though he wore a serious expression, he still ran his gaze over Thierry's naked form in appreciation then waved him over to the closet.

He thought about his morning schedule. A hearing at City Hall, which usually required a suit, would be followed by an appearance just before lunchtime at an elementary school, where he'd rather dress a bit more casually, then he had a lunch meeting with some of the city's legislators. He decided a suit to begin with and put on the pants and a shirt, then got out a cozy front-zip charcoal gray sweater he'd bring along to exchange with his jacket for the school visit. He hung it with the suit jacket on the doorknob.

When he turned around, Eduardo was holding out a blue and green striped tie with a smile.

"Not red today?" he joked, accepting it and threading it through his collar, though he left it untied for now.

"Probably be like waving a flag at a herd of bulls in the lunch meeting."

"True."

Eduardo then opened his other hand and revealed a pair of cufflinks Thierry had never seen before. He offered his first cuff to Eduardo so he could thread it through. "A gift?" he asked, touched.

"Sort of. You need to wear these every day without fail from now on." The urgency in Eduardo's voice made him look up sharply as he held up the second sleeve.

After it was fastened, he followed Eduardo over to the sitting area. "So—you first? I can tell you're dying to share something. Start with the cufflinks. Anything to do with that text?" Against his will, he yawned hard, reminding him how early it was, so he sat, grabbed his coffee and took a long drink.

Eduardo nodded his gratitude then took a deep breath before he began. "The information I was expecting through the resistance channels finally came. I met two men who came in from Ward Three with a pair of USBs." His gaze flicked meaningfully down to Thierry's sleeves then back to his face.

No way. He turned his left hand over and studied one. "Clever. And?"

"And"—Eduardo sat down—"it's even better than we hoped. Not only is there enough detail on every major player in Chicago to legitimately take them down..." Eduardo swallowed. "We finally have the proof we need regarding the real intent behind the Immigration Bill."

Noticing that his hand holding the coffee was trembling, Thierry set down the mug.

Eduardo gazed at him with sad eyes and nodded. "It's all there and we were right. Ethnic and socio-economic cleansing. The open border only swings one way. It'll start innocently enough with people who want to leave to take trips or visit outsiders, but when they come back, no re-entrance. They'll have to 'apply' for a hearing to resolve the 'irregularities' in their visa—hearings that will never happen. Meanwhile, those who are acceptable will move freely back and forth, to paint a good face on it. Soon, it'll progress to mandatory deportations, based on areas they want to take over for themselves. And at that point, if someone refuses to go, the orders are appallingly clear." Eduardo's accent, which was usually nigh to untraceable, was about as thick as Thierry had ever heard it.

Thierry knew he was thinking about his family, friends, community—the dear-to-him individuals who were about to become targets.

"That's madness."

Thierry's voice was barely audible to his own ears, but Eduardo must have heard him because he pressed his lips together.

The benignly named Immigration and Travel Bill had been put forth as a big step forward. But Thierry knew—had known for a while—that those in control of the city were not suddenly going to become altruistic. Whispers behind the scenes had told a much different story than the local media. Yet even already knowing that there was something wrong with the proposal didn't mitigate the disgust and horror Thierry felt at hearing it confirmed.

And Thierry was the public face of the governing body of Chicago. For a minute he thought he might throw up. He hung forward, conscious of his breathing, and saw Eduardo's shoes a moment before a soothing touch came to rest on his back.

"We've shared this with the resistance movement, but we have to get the information out to the outside world, to the national government. They're the only ones who can stop this." Of course, with the ridiculous separation of national and local governments, the US was handcuffed and unable to interfere except in very few specific circumstances.

Proof of a plan for wholesale genocide was probably enough…he hoped.

Eduardo knelt in front of him and took his hands. "Since you are one of the few people who can travel out of the city unimpeded, someone who has the ear of outside officials, the people who collected this information got it to me so that you can take it with you on your next trip."

"I wish I'd had it a few days ago."

"Yeah, me too. But you do have that trip next week. We just need you to keep those with you and safe" — Eduardo toyed with one of the cufflinks — "and we need to discuss who you can approach that's trustworthy and high enough up to do something about this."

Thierry nodded, his mind already racing through possibilities. The governor would be there at the event, but he couldn't trust that he wasn't involved somehow. No — it had to be someone at the national level — someone outside the sphere of influence of this area. He needed to see the schedule for the symposium to see who was speaking and who was attending. Maybe that could give him some ideas…

A sudden flurry of loud knocks on the door made them both jump. Eduardo gave him a startled look then leaped to his feet as the telltale sound of the outer room's electronic lock disengaging came. Thierry stood and they quickly crossed the bedroom. When he reached the door to the living area, Eduardo grabbed his wrist, stopping him from opening it.

"Eduardo! Mr Alexander! We need to leave, now!"

"Matt? What's going on?" Eduardo called through the door, still holding onto Thierry, though now he reached for the deadbolt.

"Do you trust him?" Thierry whispered, knowing that Eduardo's instincts about people were usually spot on. In his position as the driving force behind Chicago's resistance movement, he knew in most cases who in the mansion they could trust and who had other influences.

In answer, Eduardo grabbed the hangers off the knob, tossed the jacket to the floor and handed Thierry the sweater. "Put this on and get some shoes on. Lock it behind me." He opened the door and slipped through. "Lock it!" Eduardo slammed it closed.

Thierry hesitated a moment then did as his lover had asked. He chose black laced dress shoes instead of wingtips and hurriedly put them on, listening in vain for any sound from the outer room.

Finally a knock came followed by Eduardo's voice, "Thi. Open up."

As soon as he'd opened the door, Eduardo grabbed him by the hand and yanked him along as he ran behind the night guard—Matt, Matt... What the hell was his last name? For some random reason, it bugged Thierry that he couldn't remember it, especially now that they were dependent on the man.

"There've been at least two intruders shot inside the mansion and communications have been cut, but we don't know how many more there are, who they're here for or who they're with. We need to get you to a safe place."

"One of the safe rooms?" They were going the wrong way for that.

"We don't know who they're *with*," Eduardo stressed.

Thierry let that sink in for a moment. He was right—they needed to lie low until they had more information. "Where then?"

Matt skidded to a stop against the wall right before where the hallway came to a T. After a cautious glance around the corner, he waved them on and turned right then right again, into a seldom used guest bedroom.

Once they were inside, Matt closed the door behind them then crossed to the far side of the room. He bent down and as Thierry and Eduardo came around the foot of the bed, they could see he was struggling to lift the area rug.

Not just a rug, Thierry noted, and they moved to help the man. A concealed trapdoor camouflaged by the rug attached to it. There was a metal-runged ladder leading into darkness.

Eduardo went down first but he stopped several rungs down when Matt whispered, "Ditch your phones—anything that could be tracked." He took his own and slid it under the bed out of sight. Thierry exchanged a look with Eduardo, who nodded. He took Eduardo's, then removed his own from his pocket and followed suit.

Now they were unarmed, without phones and following a man he barely knew into a dark tunnel of some sort he'd never known about right under the executive mansion. The only thing he had to hold onto was his trust in his lover.

He took a deep breath and followed Eduardo down into the blackness.

Chapter Four

Once Matt had closed the trapdoor above them, it was so dark that Eduardo was only able to continue to move down by feel alone at first. Then he realized that his eyes were adjusting…or maybe they were getting closer to some weak source of light.

He squinted down into the darkness and could just make out a circular area below him where the rungs apparently ended. Now that he could see a little bit, he quickened his pace and jumped the last few feet to the bottom. When he ducked out from under the shaft they'd climbed down, he saw that they were in what appeared to be a utilities access tunnel. Periodic light bulbs in cages stretched off in both directions.

There was a network of tunnels in use around Chicago, most under the control of the gangs, but a few that were useful to the resistance. He'd known in theory about this particular escape route, but had hoped that they'd never have occasion to use it and call attention to it. Thierry was probably wondering what the hell was going on, and Eduardo himself had a few questions—namely, how had Matt known about it? He'd been shocked when Matt had unerringly led them to the trapdoor.

Thierry reached the ground and Eduardo stepped to the side to give him room. They were soon joined by Matt...who had his pistol drawn.

Eduardo's heart stuttered for a moment, and he grabbed Thierry and shoved him behind him, hoping to hell that he hadn't fucked up by trusting Matt. Matt wasn't focused on them, though, but on the tunnel to the left. He brushed past Eduardo without a word. Eduardo felt slightly foolish for his defensive reaction, however he'd die before allowing anything to happen to Thierry.

"We need to move quickly. I don't think anyone will be coming after us right away, but the further we can get the better." Matt began to walk down the tunnel.

"I agree." Eduardo saw the sense in that, but now that they were out of immediate danger, he wasn't about to blindly follow Matt without at least some idea of what was going on and where they were going. This tunnel system came out in several different buildings downtown. He stayed put, needing to get a few things clear before they went any farther. "Do you know where this leads?"

Matt stopped and turned around. "Yes, I do. Look, I don't want to be a dick about this, but I'm the only chance you've got right now. I know someone who can be trusted to keep you safe until we know what the hell is going on, but you have to trust me."

"We want to, so give us a name we know." Thierry's voice was steady and firm. "You must understand that we need a good reason to go with you rather than go back up to one of the safe rooms and wait it out."

Eduardo admired his lover's calm reasoning. Between the two of them and their knowledge of the players in Chicago, if Matt was on their side, he should be able to give them the name of someone they knew. Otherwise... Eduardo moved subtly in front of Thierry again.

"Fuck. Really?" Matt ran his free hand through his hair. "Fine. A first name, and only because I can see you're not going to budge until I do." He blew out a breath. "I'll admit, I get why you're paranoid. This whole city is fucked up. The guy we're going to meet is Darien."

Eduardo jolted at hearing the name of his friend who, last he'd heard, was undercover with the O'Laughlins looking into Eduardo's cousin Tomas' disappearance.

"Last initial?" he prompted, wanting to make sure it was Darien Shaunessey and not some other Darien.

Matt looked increasingly impatient. "S. Fuck! Can we go already?"

Relief surged through him. Reassured, he looked at Thierry when he responded, "Yes, let's go." His optimism seemed to assuage Thierry's wariness—he offered a small smile and nod.

The trio moved out and Matt led them for what had to be over an hour down random turns in the maze of tunnels. Obviously, he'd been briefed on the tunnel system...but by whom? Eduardo had never been down here, nor did he have any more than a vague idea of where they might come out. They passed a few metal doors and shafts similar to what they'd come down in, otherwise the tunnels were solid brick with no escape. One section was almost completely dark and left them walking slowly with Eduardo keeping a hand on Matt's shoulder, and Thierry with his finger hooked in Eduardo's belt loop. There must have been a power outage in that part of the city.

At one point Matt stopped, listened then waved them urgently into a doorwell. Following his lead, they pressed back against the door for several minutes as they heard movement up ahead. Eduardo strained his ears but thankfully the sounds didn't come any closer before they faded away. Whoever it was must have gone down another tunnel.

Matt waited silently for a few minutes after the noise had died away, then pressed his finger to his lips in an unnecessary reminder to keep quiet. He stepped back out into the tunnel then walked quickly and stealthily in the same direction the noise had been coming from.

Eduardo reached back to brush Thierry's hand. *Oh, the hell with it.* It wasn't as though there was anyone down here to see them. He linked Thierry's fingers with his and they followed. His anxiety was going through the roof, but he didn't want to lose sight of the only person who knew how to get them out of here even if it seemed he was walking straight toward some unknown person. Following him?

Matt slipped around a corner and they hustled forward as they lost sight of him…only to stop short when they almost ran into his still form.

His gun was still in his hand but pointed at the floor, and he was in a stare down with the shadowy figure of a large man standing just beyond the light of the next bulb. The fact that they seemed to outnumber the guy three to one didn't give Eduardo much satisfaction just then.

"Cesar?"

His chest seized as he unexpectedly heard his family nickname. He'd earned the nickname from Tomas after Cesar Chavez, a sort of play on his name and a gentle tease for his idealism and activism. He had never felt he had the right to the name, to be honest, hiding under the veneer of obedience instead of standing tall. Problem with Chicago was, anyone who stood tall got cut down. It was a miracle that people like Thierry were still around.

For a brief, optimistic moment he thought it might be Tomas himself, then he processed the deep voice and knew that it was the next best person.

"Dare," he broke the silence, then stepped forward.

Thierry yanked him back by the hand he was still holding, which he clamped down on so tightly that Eduardo winced. Angling toward Thierry, he tried to look into his eyes in the dim light. "It's okay," he whispered. "I trust him more than anyone besides you."

Thierry heaved a sigh then released his hand. "Sorry. This whole thing…"

"I know. Someday we'll look back and laugh."

That earned him a huff of a laugh from all three of the others. Obviously everyone was starting to come down from the high stress they'd been operating under since things had gone bad back at the mansion. Darien had taken a couple of steps forward into the light, and the sight of his friend sent Eduardo hurrying forward into his arms for a tight embrace.

"So glad to see you safe," Darien murmured in Spanish in his ear. "Do you trust the other one? Matt?" He let go of Eduardo but remained close.

"Yes," he answered without having to think about it. Matt had kept them safe, gotten Thierry away from danger and led them to his friend. Eduardo didn't hesitate to give him the stamp of approval at this point. But that made him wonder even more who had put Matt in place and given him the information he'd needed to get Thierry and Eduardo out of the mansion so quickly.

"Okay. I have someone waiting about a hundred yards down this way, who will take you to a place you can stay until we can get you out of the city. I have to get back to work before I'm missed, and I can't be seen with you by anyone. The whole point of me sending the…package the long way around was to avoid any connection between my guy and your guy." He shot a glance at Thierry then quirked his lips. "And this tunnel was a one-time shot, last resort to get your guy out of danger. Too many other friendlies know about it—it was bound to get leaked at some point. And it's likely they'll figure it out once they analyze the surveillance videos of your movements tonight and search the room. We could only use it this once without it being added to the crazy-ass surveillance network."

Eduardo frowned. Why had Darien taken the risk of coming himself? "Coming here isn't going to blow your cover, is it?" He swore softly under his breath. "Why would you do that then? Couldn't we have just met that person? If this ruined everything for you…"

"I should be okay if I get back soon. And really—would you have trusted anyone else?"

Fuck. "Okay, I get it." He ran his hand through his hair. "Let's get going then." He glanced back to see that Thierry had come to stand right behind him, with Matt at his side, listening to the hushed conversation.

They followed Darien, with Matt bringing up the rear, until they reached one of the doors. He didn't knock on the surface, but rather scratched on the bricks next to the handle. A minute later they heard a screech of metal then the door opened a crack before swinging wide to reveal a young black woman. Eduardo and Thierry hurried in, followed by Matt, but Darien stayed in the tunnel.

"Listen to Karen and stay safe. And remember"—he leaned in to speak directly to Thierry—"it's cost too many people way too much to acquire what was sent to you. Be sure you make all of their sacrifices worth it."

Thierry gave a grim nod—he obviously felt the weight of his responsibility. "Will you be all right?" he asked Dare. "We can take you with us. We're not sending you back to a bad situation, are we?"

To Eduardo's surprise, Darien grinned. "I'll be fine." His expression…softened.

It made Eduardo wonder just what had happened in his usually taciturn friend's life lately to cause that expression.

"Just do what you need to do, and we'll all be much better off." Darien gave a tip of his head then pulled the door shut, enclosing them in some sort of small room.

As he disappeared from view, Eduardo sent up a prayer that it would not be the last time he saw his friend. Karen slid a long metal bolt into place then walked a couple of steps to another door, which she rapped lightly on.

It opened and she beckoned them. "Welcome to the Waldorf Astoria Hotel."

Chapter Five

Thierry shook his head in wonder as they followed Karen through what looked like a basement to a service elevator. Who would have thought there was an underground tunnel between the executive mansion and the Waldorf Astoria? He wondered where some of the other doors led and if they'd be leaving the hotel through the tunnels again. Obviously the gangs had no idea about these particular tunnels or they'd have taken them over.

He understood the caution the people he'd seen so far had shown toward them, protecting that secret among so many others, and he vowed anew to take down the cancerous political structure that made so many people need to live in the dark and keep their secrets and contingency plans so dear.

They rode the large elevator up to thirty-four without stopping. No one spoke and Thierry belatedly wondered whether he should have disguised himself or something. He scanned for a camera but knew that they wouldn't necessarily be visible.

The doors opened and Karen led the way off the elevator. It was almost surreal to go from the dark tunnels of earlier to the luxurious hallway of the Waldorf Astoria. He'd been in this hotel many times before, actually.

They didn't meet anyone before she stopped to unlock a room for them. They walked quickly inside, into a normal one-bedroom hotel suite. Such a crazy contrast. He found himself tugging off his sweater. Evidently his subconscious was ready to settle in for the day. That, and it was warm the way that high-rise hotels got in the cold months when everyone's heat was constantly running.

Eduardo was giving him a fond smile and held out his hand for the sweater.

Thierry smacked it aside. Their respective roles were a constant source of teasing between them. "Quit it. I can hang up my own damn sweater."

Karen looked a bit startled but recovered quickly. "We put some extra toiletries in the bathroom and I'll bring up an assortment of food from room service for breakfast. Unless you'd prefer to wait for lunch…"

"Breakfast sounds great to me. Something sweet maybe," Matt spoke up, the tension missing from his voice for the first time since they'd fled the mansion. He looked tired.

Eduardo must have come to the same conclusion. "Oh, man. You've been on duty all night. You must be exhausted. Yes"—he turned to Karen—"please send up something sweet for Matt—pancakes, waffles, whatever—and a couple of omelets for us. Fruit or juice? And coffee. Lots of coffee. Soon as you can manage would be great, so Matt can get some sleep after he eats." Eduardo smiled. "We really appreciate everything you're doing for us. Thank you."

"Yes. Thank you so much." Thierry hadn't even thought about food before then but when Eduardo had rattled off the order, he'd suddenly realized that he was starving.

Once Karen was gone, the three men were left to stare at one another in the quiet, white luxury of the room. Thierry went to sit on the loveseat, automatically moving his hand to undo one of his cuffs. He stopped when he touched the cufflink — he'd almost forgotten about having them on. His gaze went to Eduardo, who was joining him, but he didn't give him any clues as to his thoughts. So he turned to Matt, studying him closely for the first time.

Matt was a bit older than he'd originally thought. Even sprawled in the chair, obviously fatigued, there was an alertness about him. He still seemed to be aware of everything that was going on and it didn't escape Thierry's notice that he'd oriented himself facing the door, with his gun in its waist holster free to his reach.

"Who are you, really?" he asked Matt. "More than just a guard — that's obvious."

Eduardo looked sharply between the two of them, but Matt didn't seem surprised by the question. He eyed Thierry, assessing him.

"I was sent here to help protect you and to extract you if necessary," he finally answered.

"So it's not a coincidence that you were always assigned to guard Thierry," Eduardo stated flatly. Rather than feeling reassured by the news that Matt was on their side and not just a friendlier-than-most guard, he looked a bit upset. Probably feeling a bit out of sorts because he hadn't figured out there was more to Matt than had appeared.

"No, it wasn't. Sorry. Though the fact that I was on duty when things went down last night was a nice bit of luck. Saved me from having to get you away from one of the other guards."

Thierry nodded. 'Extract' was a very military-sounding word, but he had the feeling that Matt had told them everything he was going to about his being here in Chicago. Instead he asked, "Did you know Darien before this?"

"No. I was just given his name when I called in for instructions on getting you two out. Good thing, too. I don't think Eduardo would have budged if I hadn't come up with it." He smiled slightly as he turned his attention to Eduardo. "You and Darien seem to know each other really well."

Eduardo tried to stop brooding over having missed Matt's hidden side while he debated how much to tell Matt about Darien. It wasn't a question, precisely, and Eduardo could have just ignored it, but he could see Thierry's interest as he also waited for his answer.

"We've known each other since we were kids."

"And he's the one who originated the information?" Thierry asked at his side.

Eduardo turned to answer him but didn't miss Matt's reaction as he sat up straighter. Thierry looked calmly at him, and Eduardo got the distinct impression that he'd included the word 'information' in front of Matt on purpose. In the tunnel, they'd only ever referred to a 'package'.

"Not exactly," Eduardo finally answered. "I mean, he's the one who put things into motion to get it to us through the resistance, but it was someone else who assembled it all. Took years, from what I heard."

"Do you know who?" Thierry frowned.

Eduardo shrugged, not really wanting to see his lover's reaction if he were to reveal that it was the son of one of the worst crime families. "Does it matter?"

Thierry appeared to consider that for a minute. "Well, I'd like to think that the person who did it really wants to effect change without having an ulterior motive that might have tainted the info. But then again, who am I to say what's a 'right' reason?" Thierry bent to unlace his shoes, and Eduardo knew that he was giving himself time to think without his expression being open to scrutiny. "I also don't like to think of this person being harmed if it becomes apparent what he or she has done to help us. Or if there's some blowback that we could protect them from." He sat up and his troubled expression made Eduardo sigh.

"It was one of the O'Laughlins," he admitted quietly.

"What?" came the disbelieving chorus from Thierry and Matt.

A knock at the door brought them all back around. Eduardo barely beat Matt to his feet. "I'll get it."

Matt followed him to the door but restrained himself from actually shoving Eduardo aside and looking out of the peephole himself. "Only open it for Karen," Matt cautioned.

It was Karen in the fish-eyed view, with a room service cart, so he undid the locks and let her push it inside. "Anything else you guys need?" she asked.

"I think we should be fine for now." Oh God, the coffee smelled good. Eduardo hadn't even gotten a sip of his this morning before things had gone crazy.

"I've left my direct extension number and my cell number on the tray. Call me if anything comes up. This room is rented under a pseudonym, so try not to call attention to yourselves. I'd avoid leaving the room, but you're not prisoners, of course." Karen's cell phone chimed and she glanced down. "I have to go, but you have my number."

"Thank you." Eduardo walked her to the door and locked up behind her.

Matt had wheeled the cart closer to the coffee table in the sitting area and was already taking covers off the plates. "I don't know about you two, but I'm ready to do this justice. Holy crow." He'd just revealed a huge Belgian waffle with strawberries on top. "You guys were good with the omelets, right?"

Thierry laughed and the lighthearted sound was so great to hear. "Go ahead, it's all yours." He grinned at Eduardo. "You hungry…?" The inquiry trailed off and Eduardo could almost hear the endearment he'd omitted at the end.

He had no idea how long they'd be here until they were moved again, so they might as well get comfortable and fed. "Yeah. Let's eat."

Chapter Six

The three men had eaten every bite of food and now Matt was getting some much needed rest, fast asleep still clothed on the pull-out loveseat. They'd offered him the bedroom as he was the one who needed sleep the most, but he'd declined, saying that he wanted to be closer to the door. Thierry suspected that in addition to that, Matt knew the two of them wouldn't be averse to sharing the bedroom.

"Come here," Eduardo said softly.

Thierry crossed the room and took his hand, giving a light tug that brought his lover into his arms.

"Why don't we lie down for a while? Who knows when we'll have a chance again?" Eduardo pressed Thierry back on his chest to separate them then began to undo one of the cufflinks.

"Should I just keep them on?" Thierry asked.

"We'll put them in your pants." Eduardo winked.

"Oh, so I guess the pants are coming off too, then."

"Yes, definitely." The other cufflink was undone and Eduardo tucked them into Thierry's front left pocket, making sure to cop a feel in the process that had Thierry hardening even further.

They finished undressing and Thierry put the clothes on the dresser so they'd be handy in case they had to dress in a hurry.

"You should hang up your shirt so it doesn't wrinkle."

Thierry laughed softly. "I think it's too late, but hey—I have a pretty good excuse. Being on the run isn't easy on clothes. I'm just glad that was a utility access tunnel and not a sewer."

"Only the best for you," Eduardo joked as he pulled down the covers. He climbed into bed and Thierry wasted no time in joining him.

When he took Eduardo into his arms, his hard cock pressed along Eduardo's abdomen, but there was no corresponding hardness against him.

"Not in the mood?" he whispered, ignoring his erection and settling Eduardo in his embrace.

"Oh, I'm always in the mood for you. Just need a little time to catch up. Lot on my mind."

"Matt?"

"Yeah. I'm not happy that I didn't know about him, and still a bit worried about how much information is out there. I guess that's a silly thing to worry about— it's good that people outside of Chicago know and care enough to get people in here to help. I just…"

"You don't like being out of the loop."

Eduardo nodded against his shoulder.

"Imagine how I feel." Thierry sighed, then decided to lighten the mood. "You don't have to just imagine, you know. You can actually feel me."

Raising himself up until he could look straight at Thierry, Eduardo gave him an incredulous look. "Okay, that was just bad."

"Hey, a guy can hope." Thierry ran his hand down Eduardo's back to his firm ass.

"Mmm." Eduardo arched and pressed against his hand. "I like all this talk of feeling. And the actual touching part too."

A thought occurred to him. "I hate to spoil the party, but I'm pretty sure Karen didn't leave us lube or condoms."

Eduardo froze then groaned. "Crap."

Thierry squeezed his ass then rolled out of the bed, heading to the bathroom. He returned triumphant, waggling the small bottle of lotion at Eduardo. "Lotion should work for something fun, even if we can't fuck."

"We could try..." Technically they could. They'd been monogamous for close to three years after they'd met on the campaign trail. It had been attraction at first glance, one of the few times Thierry had gone with his instincts rather than playing it safe. He'd been thankful every day since that Eduardo had seen something in him in return.

Meant to be.

He squeezed quite a bit of lotion into his hand and sniffed it reflexively. Sort of minty and herby. He settled back into the bed and pulled Eduardo up against him "Nah. We can do this." He adjusted his position until he could grasp both of their erections in one hand, with his thumb under his shaft and fingers curled around Eduardo's. "This'll be good." It was already good, and he'd only given them a couple of strokes.

Once he'd spread the lotion around, he met Eduardo's mouth in a tender kiss that quickly deepened as he worked their cocks. Eduardo hugged him close with his top arm, and Thierry barely had room to move his hand. But that only added to the intimacy, giving their cock heads pressure between them when they pressed out of the top of his fist on the downstroke.

They swallowed each other's breath and gasps of pleasure as Thierry brought them quickly to the edge. Eduardo went first, which Thierry was grateful for, and his warm ejaculate aided the glide of his hand. Then Eduardo batted it away and used his cum to ruthlessly pull Thierry's orgasm from him.

He slammed his mouth back down on Thierry's just in time to muffle his shout as he came hard. Eduardo moaned into his mouth in response, and softened his grip just in time before Thierry's cock became too sensitive. It was as though he had a sixth sense about it—that or they were perfectly suited to one another.

Rather than get up, Thierry stripped a pillowcase off one of the multitude of pillows and used it to swipe at their hands, abdomens and the sheets before rolling Eduardo over to the cleaner side of the bed. He sighed.

"You okay?" Eduardo pulled the sheet up over them then lay with his arm across Thierry's stomach.

"Just thinking about what to do now. Don't get me wrong. I'm glad we got out of there when we did, especially with what you received, but all the slinking around really goes against my grain. I don't want to be a rat in the gutter, like them."

Eduardo stroked his naked chest thoughtfully. "*Mi abuela* used to say, the good people of the world—like you—they got an extra light in their heart. Shines out of them, and if it's protected, it grows higher and stronger and shows other people the way. It can be vulnerable, though." Pain turned his reminiscent smile into a grimace. "My cousin Tomas was like that—he had that flame of goodness deep inside. God, if he's"—he took a shuddering breath—"still alive, I hope and pray he was able to shelter that part of him. Bank it down so it's not out forever."

Thierry was riveted by the raw emotion on his lover's face. He ached with the need to pull Eduardo in and kiss away his troubles, but he instinctively knew that Eduardo needed to get this out without a gesture that might cause him to lose his tenuous grip on his control.

"And you…" Eduardo swallowed heavily but didn't continue right away.

Thierry prompted quietly, "You think I have this light?"

He was shocked when Eduardo snorted then gave a laugh. "You? You don't have a light, man. You have a fucking bonfire of goodness in your heart." Sincerity shone from Eduardo, causing goosebumps of want and something else to race through Thierry.

Eduardo pulled back a bit, bracing himself up on one elbow, and Thierry shivered as he finished by whispering in his ear, his breath skating against his skin, "And that's why you are meant to be the one to lead us out of the darkness. And that's why you will succeed." Eduardo's voice lowered to a rumble as he slid his hand along Thierry's jaw. "And that's why I love you."

It was the first time Thierry had heard those words from Eduardo, and it seemed so right and necessary now, in the wake of what was changing around them and the hope of what was to come.

And it made Thierry's decision about what to do next crystal clear.

Chapter Seven

"You are fucking crazy," Eduardo said flatly. Ever since Thierry had announced his plan for getting out of Chicago with the information, Eduardo had been trying to convince him to change his mind, but he could tell that his lover's mind was set.

Matt was nodding his agreement, though a tinge of admiration shone through in his eyes. "You know this is going to tempt them to take you out for good."

"Why can't we do it our way and once you're safely out, then you can grandstand and call them out? Why do you have to rub it in their faces?" Eduardo ran his hand over his hair.

Karen watched them all with an inscrutable expression. She'd come back up a short time earlier with the news that they'd arranged to have Thierry go back down through the tunnel to the farthest point, have resistance members there help him with a disguise, ID and forged papers, then smuggle him out of Chicago.

Thierry had adamantly refused to disguise himself, sneak out of the city, or even wait until dark. Instead, he'd explained that he was going to hold a small press conference right in the damn courtyard of the hotel before getting in a car and driving bold as brass right out of the city.

He'd lost his freaking mind.

Thierry sighed, but it didn't sound frustrated—more like he was gathering strength. "I need to do this the right way. If I sneak out, I'm down at their level like a rat in the sewer. Either that or I'm cowering. Cowed by their threats." His eyes pleaded with Eduardo for understanding. "You of all people understand about giving people hope. You've been doing your part for years now. It's time for me to do mine—use the position I'm in to get the people of this city to a better place. Bad as it's been, it'll get much, much worse if they're not stopped...*right now*," Thierry emphasized.

"Have the press conference after you're out," he argued. "It'll be a matter of hours. What's the difference?"

"It'll be a matter of miles," Thierry countered. "I can pass through the border, but so many people can't. I want to do this here, in our city. They deserve for me to begin the end here."

It made some sense, particularly the point about giving people hope. That would be especially important to his resistance members, who could then lead the populace. "Fuck."

Thierry took his hands and held them firmly. "We need to do this together, Cesar."

A gasp came from Karen, and they all turned in her direction.

"You're Cesar." She was clearly astonished and suddenly shot to her feet. "I'll be right back." Before they could stop her, she was out of the door, leaving the three men staring at one another.

"I really hope that wasn't a bad move, revealing your presence here." Thierry finally released Eduardo's hands. "You've been the figurehead for the resistance for so long, and I'm sure that part of that longevity was due to your anonymity."

Eduardo chewed that over in his head for a few moments. "Like it or not, things are in motion. No going back now." He looked at Matt, who was nodding in agreement. "So, I suppose we need to arrange some press we can count on."

Thierry gave him that charismatic, genuine smile that had endeared him to the whole city…and had made Eduardo fall in love with him. "Yes, and a car and driver for afterward. Someone we can trust and who is willing to leave the city."

Matt shrugged. "Get me a car and I could do it. I'll be going with you either way."

That made Eduardo recall the pair from Three that he'd arranged to go underground until he could get them out of the city. "Actually, I have someone in mind. Two guys, since I'm pretty sure the one won't go without the other. Let me make some calls." He'd need to get in touch with his most reliable staff member to arrange for Dirk and Leon to pick up a car and come to the hotel. He began mentally sorting through press contacts, his head spinning.

After making a few phone calls, he had enough arranged to give him some cautious hope that things might work out. If they were lucky.

The door opened and they all froze when Karen came back in, followed by a short, Hispanic man in a bellhop's uniform. Karen pointed at Eduardo and whispered into the young man's ear then patted his shoulder.

"You are Cesar?" he hesitantly asked in Spanish.

Eduardo couldn't read any threat in the man before him. "Yes. And you are...?"

"I'm nobody, but I have a message for you." He reached into his pocket and pulled out a folded, battered piece of paper. After handing it to Eduardo, he stepped back then turned and headed to the door.

"Wait," Eduardo called out.

But the man slipped out of the room, followed by Karen, who held up a finger as if to say she'd be right back.

He gently opened the note and began to read. The note was in Spanish and in a tantalizingly familiar handwriting.

Cesar – I am okay for now but if this finds you, I am in Springfield, at the very top. I don't have any way to leave but I can be seen at the best address.
Love and miss you, Tomas

He brought his hand to his mouth then wordlessly handed the note to Thierry, who scanned it. "I can't read Spanish. What is it?" His gaze sharpened. "Tomas? This is from your cousin?"

Karen slipped back into the room and Eduardo immediately went to her. "Where did that man go? I need to talk to him."

She shook her head. "He doesn't know much. The note was brought into Chicago by his friend about a year ago, who left the city once he gave it to him. He hasn't seen or heard from him since."

"A year?" A lot could happen in a year. Still, it was the first contact they'd had—the first clear indication that Tomas was still alive, or had been a year ago. He read the note out loud, then thought for a minute. "Springfield. At the top? Best address. What—?"

"Either the Capitol or the governor's mansion." Thierry sounded very sure, and Eduardo could have smacked his forehead.

Of course.

"It's a starting point." He refused to allow himself get too excited then face disappointment.

"Yes." Thierry grasped his shoulder. "And we can start there once we do what we need to do for Chicago."

"Right." Eduardo tried to push his cousin's situation out of his mind. They had more pressing issues at the moment. "Okay, let's get you ready, Mr Deputy Mayor."

* * * *

The courtyard was a lovely setting, and with only two camera crews and a few reporters, it was actually rather peaceful, but Thierry was mindful that he wasn't just addressing the half dozen people there, but all the residents of his city.

"And so," he concluded, "I am committed to restoring and preserving freedom for the people of Chicago, not in the ruse of the 'Bill' of goods you're being sold, but with the rights that apply equally to all. I will speak to you again in a few days' time. Thank you for allowing me to serve you and this beautiful city." He smiled for the cameras and lifted a hand in a hail as he strode toward the waiting car, ignoring the shouted questions from the reporters.

One of the men from Three—Dirk—held the door for him and as soon as he was inside, he closed it behind him. The press had moved forward and Dirk wove through them to get to the driver's door and join his partner Leon, who was already sitting up front.

Matt and Eduardo were riding in the back with Thierry.

Thierry breathed deeply for the first time in a long time as the car set in motion.

"You sounded great." Eduardo patted his knee.

"Thanks. I—" He cleared his throat. "I hope I'm doing the right thing."

"You are," Matt jumped in to say from the seat across from them. "I can't imagine why you wouldn't think so, considering what these monsters were planning to do."

"What I'm doing might take some of these guys down, but who's to say someone worse won't fill the vacuum?" Thierry voiced his biggest fear.

"You know—it's possible that might happen. I can't predict the future. But I hope and feel that it will get better." Eduardo gazed at him reassuringly. "We'll make sure of it. You and me…and everyone who believes in a better Chicago."

The privacy window went down a crack and Leon turned around in the passenger's seat. "We're going into the main south border crossing and it looks like we might have company." They were driving toward Midway Airport, all in agreement that flying out of the city was the best tactic. However, to get there they'd have to cross into Five—not usually a problem for Thierry with his credentials, but…

"The mayor is here."

Damn it. "All right. Pull up as far as you can in the VIP lane then stop the car."

They crawled forward, and it seemed that people and cars were all around them, many more than usual. Had their enemies somehow guessed their route? The last thing Thierry wanted was a public fight or the start to a riot.

He focused on the mayor's car, and sure enough, saw the man standing there flanked by several police officers.

When he reached for the car door, Eduardo grabbed him. "No way. You can't go out there. He'll either have you arrested or shot."

"He won't do that," Thierry replied, thankfully sounding more confident than he felt. "There are press here." He pointed toward news vans with satellite dishes.

Eduardo shook his head. "I don't care. He'll find some way to do it."

"It's okay." Past caring about their audience, he leaned forward and brushed a kiss across Eduardo's lips. "Either way, it'll be okay." He quickly got out before Eduardo could stop him.

"Thi!" Eduardo's cry was almost drowned out by a cacophony of sound as the gathered crowed saw him emerge.

The loud cheering caught him off guard but he raised his hand in response, then took a deep breath and walked straight toward the mayor.

"You are out of your mind," the mayor ground out when he got close enough to hear.

"That's the second time today I've been accused of that. But *your* opinion? I could care less about." He tried not to think about the slight weight of the cufflinks at his wrists, covered by the sleeves of his sweater. "Stand aside. This is over and you know it."

"Who are you to tell me what to do?" the mayor sneered then turned to the police officer next to him. "Detain him."

The officer, a large, middle-aged man, looked between the two leaders, then to one of the other policemen. He all but shrugged. "I have no reason to detain him, Mr Mayor."

"Well, come up with something! I'm sure someone in his car is illegal. And he's inciting a riot." The furious mayor waved his hand at the crowd around them.

The officer addressed Thierry, "Sir, you can tell your driver to move forward."

"What? I'll have your badge for this! Who is your superior officer?"

Thierry turned around and walked away, head held high. He kept his face pleasant and nodded to some of the people he passed. A somewhat familiar face caught his eye.

Darien, Eduardo's friend from the tunnel, nodded at him but didn't say anything as he passed, just stood amid the crowd watching him go by. His being there made Thierry consider the people a bit more carefully. Were they all part of Cesar's resistance group? No — not all of them, that wasn't possible, but the word was obviously going out since the crowd kept growing.

When he reached the car, Eduardo came flying out of the back. "What the hell? I swear, you are in so much trouble. You could have been killed." He tugged him back into the car, but Thierry turned and gave one more wave before relenting.

Dirk set out slowly, and when they reached the booth, the border guard didn't even make them stop — just waved them through.

Thierry exhaled then smiled and turned to Eduardo, who was muttering in Spanish under his breath. He grasped his face between his hands, stilling him. "It's going to be okay. All of it. I *know* it. Believe me."

Eduardo took a shuddering breath, his dark eyes glistening up at Thierry. He was obviously almost at the breaking point. "I believe *in* you."

"You believed in Chicago—in all of us, Cesar—and that's why we're here in this moment." He kissed him lightly then pulled back. "There's a lot of work ahead for us, but having you there makes everything worth it. I'm a lucky man." He could sense Eduardo was ready to protest so he leaned in and kissed him breathless instead.

"*You* are the one with the bonfire heart," he murmured against Eduardo's lips, and it seemed entirely fitting that a fire would be what would save Chicago.

Epilogue

Two weeks later

"The city of Chicago remains under martial law today following the riot of two weeks ago, with National Guard troops partnering with local law enforcement to suppress any reactions from the citizenry after the successful impeachment of the city's mayor. The former Deputy Mayor Thierry Alexander was officially sworn in as his successor today in a well-attended public ceremony on the steps of the executive mansion. Thus far tonight, the city remains peaceful.

"In other news, a major ATF sting operation has so far resulted in the arrests of hundreds in the city. An anonymous source working in partnership with government agencies has helped in exposing the major players in drug and weapons distribution, as well as rampant corruption in the judicial system. Investigations are ongoing and expected to continue as new information comes to light.

"Mayor Alexander has remained a visible and positive symbol of a new start for Chicago over the past two weeks.

His memorable and heartfelt pleas to the residents of Chicago to desist from rioting went viral and made him recognizable around the world. Pundits foresee a bright political future for him, and have him making a run at the governor's office during the next election." The anchor smiled as she came up for air to sum up the lead story. *"He will certainly have quite a following if he decides to run. Back with sports after this."*

"Can we turn this off already?" Thierry grumbled as he finished fastening his belt buckle.

Eduardo ruffled his hair then hit the power button to the TV. Since the reception was a private event, Thierry had wanted to change out of his inaugural suit, ostensibly to appear more accessible, but Eduardo knew that he had just needed a bit of quiet, some time away from the spotlight he'd been living under since everything had broken open.

"Sure. We need to make your big entrance now anyway, now that you've had a moment to breathe." He leaned in to kiss Thierry's cheek, resting against his arm, and lingered to breathe in his familiar scent. It had been an extremely busy, though rewarding, time for them.

Thierry stopped fussing with his mussed hair and turned to take him in his arms. "Need a hug?"

"Probably as much as you do," Eduardo admitted, enjoying the firm embrace.

"Yeah. Thanks for everything." He kissed him briefly on the mouth. "You were such a major part of turning things around, and you don't even get any of the credit."

"I don't need it. You know that doesn't matter to me." It really didn't. Eduardo was more suited to working behind the scenes, and he was very certain of

Thierry's appreciation and support. They made a great team.

"I know." Thierry gave him one last squeeze then stepped back. "How do I look?"

"Very mayoral," he teased.

"Very funny." Thierry's face relaxed a bit and Eduardo grinned.

They walked out of the suite then descended to the ballroom, where the carefully chosen inaugural guests had gathered. The party was well under way and the hum of conversations got louder the closer they got.

"Ready?" Eduardo asked as they paused in the foyer outside the tall, open doors.

Thierry just nodded and took a deep breath before he strode into the room.

Applause immediately went up and built as people took notice of his entrance. Eduardo slipped inside behind him and let him have his moment.

"Thanks for the invitation," was murmured in his ear in Spanish.

Eduardo cocked his head to glance at Darien. "Thanks for coming. Sorry about the whole fiasco." At the last minute after the final list had been developed, there had been a huge security issue. During the routine screening of guests, the spotlight had turned on Darien and his lover Farris, part of the O'Laughlin crime family. It had taken a concerted intervention from Thierry to not only get them approved for attendance, but also to move up their depositions to the government agent to exonerate them once and for all from their O'Laughlin associations. "Where's Farris? I wanted to meet him."

"He's still hiding in the washroom, I think. First, can I introduce you to some of your guys?" Darien offered quietly.

Eduardo glanced at Thierry, who was surrounded by well-wishers, and nodded. He was looking forward to meeting the men who had taken Farris' information from Darien and started the dangerous task of getting it to Thierry.

He followed Darien as he moved easily through the crowded room toward four men who were standing and talking near the corner. It was an emotional moment for Eduardo, approaching these men who had risked so much to save their city from their respective wards, and who could all now move freely around the city.

Dirk and Leon had also been invited, but had declined. They'd moved on after leaving the city with Eduardo, Matt and Thierry, and had no desire to return to Chicago any time soon. Matt had been at the inauguration, but tonight had begged off the reception. His team was hard at work in the middle of the feds' investigation, trying to completely eradicate the gang system so it didn't spring back up.

Darien greeted the men from the resistance. "Hey, guys." All eyes focused on them as they joined the circle. "I wanted to introduce you to the second most important man in the room."

Eduardo rolled his eyes at Darien. "Seriously?"

His friend grinned at him. "This is Eduardo Chavez Morales, one of my oldest friends in the world." He paused. "But you all know him better as Cesar."

"Holy crap," the shortest of the men exclaimed. The taller dark-haired man close by him also wore a look of surprise, which he quickly hid.

"Cesar..." A third man recovered and offered his hand. "Moran Schultz. I can't believe I'm meeting you in person. Thank you so much—you made it so I didn't have to leave my brother. I just…" He trailed off, looking emotional.

An imposing bald man was the only one who hadn't visibly reacted to Darien's introduction. He gently patted Moran on the shoulder then offered his hand to Eduardo. "Dutch."

Eduardo nodded in recognition and shook his hand. They'd dealt together for such a long time that he felt he already knew him. He smiled at the pair then turned to the other two men as Darien introduced them, "And these two are Georgio and Tito."

The younger one, Tito, was clearly in awe. The quiet one, Georgio, was evidently a good friend of Dirk and a brother to the twins who'd run Three. He had the look of a man who'd seen too much, probably not helped by the news that his brothers had been killed during the uprising a couple of weeks before that had happened as they'd left the city with the USBs. Eduardo had no idea whether or not the three brothers had been on decent terms, but it had to have affected him.

Resistance members had taken the opportunity after Thierry had given his speech to make a brave and concerted move against the gangs, citywide. 'Riots' they'd been termed by the media, but it was far from an unruly mob making trouble—more like people working together to take back their lives.

No one knew for sure who had taken out the twins, but the one intercepted message referring to it had contained a female pronoun.

"Thank you all," Eduardo said simply, not knowing what else to say that would do all of their efforts justice. He looked at each of them in turn, pausing when his gaze landed on a tall but somewhat fragile-looking man, still wearing his heavy outer jacket, who'd silently come to stand next to Darien. He was unmistakably an O'Laughlin. "You must be Farris."

His smile was genuine, if slightly bitter. "I've heard a lot about you."

At first Eduardo thought he meant from Darien, then it occurred to him that this was the man who'd been Tomas' lover. He wondered if Darien had shared the information they'd received in the note from Tomas.

"You know what that means about Springfield," Farris said as though reading Eduardo's mind. Farris cut a vicious side-eye across the room toward the governor, who was standing at the bar. "Doesn't surprise me, in retrospect. He's always been tight with my father and brother."

Eduardo pressed his lips together. "We're heading down there next week, and we'll see what we can find out. The note is a year old, so—"

"He's still there," Farris interrupted flatly. "That's why I actually came tonight—this really isn't my scene. But I got an email today from a former crazy-house resident I'm still in touch with. He's nutty as fuck but one of those guys with perfect recall. He spotted him in the background of some video coverage of a press conference by the governor last week. I'll forward it to you."

Eduardo's heartbeat sped up. Finally some concrete proof that Tomas was alive and at least well enough to be seen in public. He forced his excitement down. There was obviously some reason Tomas hadn't been able to contact anyone in the family, but at least they now had some hope.

A hand resting on his shoulder made him exhale. He knew instinctively that it was Thierry behind him from the feel of his presence and his scent, but the expressions of respect from the other men would have been a dead giveaway.

"Eduardo. Everything okay?"

He shot his lover a grateful look. He must have noticed Eduardo's disquiet during the discussion about Tomas from across the room and rushed over to check on him.

"Better than okay. Farris O'Laughlin has some good news for us that will help with our trip next week."

"Ah." Thierry studied him for a moment then reached out to shake Farris' hand. "It seems we have a lot to thank you for."

Farris gave a snort.

Eduardo knew from Darien that Farris' part in bringing down Chicago's gangs was almost entirely motivated by the revenge he wanted on his brother, who'd had him committed and had made his lover Tomas disappear. But it was also true that without that passion for vengeance, they could never have broken the system.

Darien intervened, waving a waiter with a tray of drinks over. "Let's have a toast."

Everyone chose a glass, and Darien held his aloft. "Here's to Mayor Alexander."

"No," Thierry interjected. "To you and Farris for getting this going."

Tito spoke up. "Cesar. To Cesar."

Eduardo smiled and held up a hand. "Let's make this simpler. To Chicago."

At his side, Thierry clinked his glass. "Chicago."

"Chicago," the other men echoed, even Farris.

They touched glasses all around, and Eduardo took a sip of the bubbly wine, amazed and gratified that this moment had been able to happen at all. "Hear, hear."

About the Authors

T.A. Chase

There is beauty in every kind of love, so why not live a life without boundaries? Experiencing everything the world offers fascinates TA and writing about the things that make each of us unique is how she shares those insights. When not writing, TA's watching movies, reading and living life to the fullest.

Jambrea Jo Jones

Jambrea wanted to be the youngest romance author published, but life impeded the dreams. She put her writing aside and went to college briefly, then enlisted in the Air Force. After serving in the military, she returned home to Indiana to start her family. A few years later, she discovered yahoo groups and book reviews. There was no turning back. She was bit by the writing bug.

She enjoys spending time with her son when not writing and loves to receive reader feedback. She's addicted to the internet so feel free to email her anytime.

Stephani Hecht

Stephani Hecht is a happily married mother of two. Born and raised in Michigan, she loves all things about the state, from the frigid winters to the Detroit Red Wings hockey team. You can usually find her snuggled up to her laptop, creating her next book.

Amber Kell

Amber Kell has made a career out of daydreaming. It has been a lifelong habit she practices diligently as shown by her complete lack of focus on anything not related to her fantasy world building.

When she told her husband what she wanted to do with her life he told her to go have fun.

During those seconds she isn't writing she remembers she has children who humor her with games of 'what if' and let her drag them to foreign lands to gather inspiration. Her youngest confided in her that he wants to write because he longs for a website and an author name—two things apparently necessary to be a proper writer.

Despite her husband's insistence she doesn't drink enough to be a true literary genius she continues to spin stories of people falling happily in love and staying that way.

She is thwarted during the day by a traffic jam of cats on the stairway and a puppy who insists on walks, but she bravely perseveres.

Devon Rhodes

Devon started reading and writing at an early age and never looked back. At 39 and holding, Devon finally figured out the best way to channel her midlife crisis was to morph from mild-mannered stay-at-home mom to erotic romance writer. She lives in Oregon with her family, who are (mostly) understanding of all the time she spends on her laptop, aka the black hole.

All of the above authors love to hear from readers. You can find their contact information, website details and author profile pages at http://www.totallybound.com.

Totally Bound Publishing